The
RING
TREE
MURDERS

By

Mel Herbert

1st edition 2024

ISBN numbers:

979-8-9900627-3-3 (paperback)

979-8-9900627-4-0 (ePub)

979-8-9900627-5-7 (audiobook)

Book Cover design and typesetting by CoverKitchen

Illustrations by Jaye Weiner

Contents

Prologue: Gone   1

The River   3

Vanished   11

Brett   15

The Torture   21

The Long Walk   27

The Lost Girl   41

Norah's House   55

The Picture and the Plan   63

Back at the Ring Tree   79

The Other Place   87

Ava in Wonderland   95

Reunion   101

The Shed on the Hill   113

Family, Stories, and Horses   121

The Lie   127

Little Traveler and the Rescue   135

Albert   143

The Witches of Equestrian   151

The Priest   165

The Chase   171

Home Again   187

Epilogue   195

Notes and Disclaimers   201

About the Author   203

To my wonderful wife, Mary,
and remarkable son, Micah
(Micah, this is 15 years late in coming,
written with your younger self in mind
-Dad)

The Ring Tree is a site of particular cultural or religious significance to the indigenous people of Australia. Representing a boundary or a place of ancient lore, these trees are formed by the young, supple branches fused together using string woven from reeds. Ring trees can live for hundreds of years.

Prologue: Gone

"She's gone! Oh my God, she's gone!" Ivy's mother screamed into the night with all the pain of an insight that is too much to bear. "My girl has gone, what have I done? First one, then the other!"

Across the paddock, down by the river, curled in a ball on the still-warm ground, a girl wept tears of deep sadness but also relief. Great fear but also great hope filled her small body. Her tears fell for a life that was over, and in fear and excitement for what was yet to come.

This place, this horrible and yet beautiful place, was home to a great mystery lost in the years past, lost from a people long gone from this land. Yet the mystery remained. They had rediscovered it, and now her soulmate, her dear friend, the sharer of the secret, was indeed gone.

This is their story.

The River

The land was hot, dry, and dusty. The Australian land-scape was unmistakable, with its red and brown dirt, low-lying weeds, tumble weeds everywhere, and kanga-roos. Those majestic, hypnotic animals that somehow only evolved on the Australian continent. They bounded togeth-er like a rhythmic drum beat, up and down, so smooth and fluid one could not look away. One started, then another joined, then another, until the entire mob moved seamlessly over the land in a wave-like flow that went up and down, up and down.

Looking on, with their distinctive cry that sounded like laughter, the kookaburras were always looking, always see-ing, always laughing, sometimes maniacally. They were the sentries at the gate, never seeming to sleep, observing all, warning all, blending in. Hidden except when they choose not to be, the kookaburra had ancient significance in Aus-tralia, representing strength, courage, freedom, family, intelligence, and protection. Most importantly, it was be-lieved their laughter could return lost souls to their families.

Here in this place grew two young girls, both thirteen years old, both born of the country, both bound to the country. Coated with the dirt, filled with the sounds and smells and sights of this magnificent land. Bound together as much as they were bound to the place. Cousins thrown together by tragedy, two becoming as one.

For them this place was not all beauty and majesty. In this place were hard and very dark places too. Together, they moved through the land, not just on it but through it, part of it, nurtured and expanded by it.

Casting a shadow over that land was the house. It sat on a hill overlooking the paddocks and the animals. It stood in silence, but it told a story, keeping that story tight within its walls, doing its best not to let it leak out. The girls knew the story, as it was part of them. They, too, kept it close; they, too, were part of that story. A story they would choose to forget if they could, a story they would like to leave behind if they could, a story they would like to change if it were possible. But it was theirs, nevertheless.

This day, like every day almost from the time they could walk, the two girls roamed the land. The hot sun beat down but the shade of the eucalyptus trees and the breeze from the river kept them a little cooler. The land was vast, especially to ones so young, seeming to go on forever. They were allowed to roam as they pleased, only having to return at dusk, and even then, if they did not, they were likely not discovered until long after dark.

They lived on an old cattle and sheep farm, but long gone were the cattle and sheep. Years of drought and mismanagement had seen them leave this place and give it back to the natives: the kangaroos, the snakes, and the rabbits—not so native, but so many. The land was reforming itself into the old times, the time before this time, the time of the others.

Through this land ran a river that had flowed from the beginning of the time of men. It had changed course, made billabongs, almost completely dried up, and reformed, but it was always there, always watching, always seeing. The river was a beautiful and dangerous place. It had taken the lives of many who took it for granted, with its whirlpools, water caverns, and submerged trees. There were also river snakes that called it home. Wonderfully terrifying creatures that glided across the water but with one bite could fell the largest of men, let alone the smallest of children.

It was just a year earlier that the girls had lost friends to this river.

* * *

"Brett, don't jump off that, please! We'll get in trouble!" Ivy cried.

Brett was also thirteen and lived on a farm as well. He was in their class at the local school. His land was next to theirs and the three would meet at the banks of the river and play their games and dream their dreams. Brett was big, the biggest of the kids in the class, with curly blond hair. Not yet a man, but about to become one.

On this day, Brett was full of energy and something more than just that. There was a sadness to him. The girls saw this often but it usually passed. He, too, lived in one of those homes on a hill.

"What are you so afraid of? No one can see us! Don't you want to just jump in? We never swim here, right here, in this river!" he cried from the broken tree now lying halfway in the river.

"Please, don't," pleaded Ava, "Remember how Ivyonny Greg died last year in the river? It's too dangerous!"

"Ivyonny jumped off the town bridge! Ivyonny was a total dickhead. Who jumps off a bridge?" Brett lamented.

"He was trying to save that kid, what's his name, that little kid?" Ava argued.

"My brother was there and said that was bullshit! That kid was just playing in the water and Ivyonny wanted to impress the girls so he pretended the kid was drowning and jumped in to 'save' him!" Brett yelled. "I'm not jumping off a bridge, I'm jumping off an old log! Just to cool off. It's so hot! Come on, come with me! Let's all jump in together, we can make a pact, we'll never tell anyone!"

Ivy joined in. "Please, Brett, no! We'll get in so much trouble if our parents find out! I don't want to get in trouble anymore. Please don't, please?" She was in tears now.

"Don't be a baby, Ivy! You'll get in trouble anyway, you always do, even when you don't do anything wrong, so why not do something worth getting in trouble for? I'm doing it, I'm going in!"

And with that, he jumped.

To Ava and Ivy, he seemed to be suspended in mid-air for the longest time, like a slow-motion camera had caught him in the moment, his blond hair glistening in the sun, that cheeky smile radiating from his face. The face of a man, not a boy. The face that seemed already worn with years beyond his years.

Then, *boom*, the reel sped up and he disappeared into the water.

Ava and Ivy, without realizing it, held their breath waiting for Brett to come up. But he did not come up. One second, two, three—where was he? Four, five, six. Panic was all around them, inside of them, over them.

Ivy started to scream out his name when, suddenly, Brett burst through the water with a maniacal laugh. "Ha-haha! I got you!" he cried.

Ava yelled, "That is *not* funny, Brett! Don't be a dickhead! That was really scary!" She could barely hold in the tears.

"Come on in! It's so cold, but you get used to it really fast," Brett declared.

"Please, get out, Brett! Please," Ava pleaded. She was the adventurous one, with long blond hair and freckles. The one you could not stop, the one who always defined the rules. She was the one most likely to jump in the river, but not this river, not this place. "Please, Brett, just get out! You're scaring us and we'll get in so much trouble!" she pleaded once more.

There was a look in Brett's eye, a twinkle, that boys get when they are tormenting girls they like. A response, any response, is what they are looking for and he was getting it. Like all thirteen-year-old boys, he did not know when to stop. It was too delicious, too powerful, just too much fun.

"Well, I'm going to swim to the other side. We've never been over there and I'm going to be the first, the first explorer of a new land, like Burke and Wills!'' Brett proclaimed.

Ava had to laugh at this, despite her panic. "They died, you know, or didn't you get to that part because you can't read!"

She immediately regretted it, immediately felt ashamed, because it was a secret. Brett could not read. Well, at least not much, and only the three of them knew. He kept it secret because he had the best memory of any of them and could hear a story once and remember it word for word, but he could never read ahead to see what happened next.

Brett gave her a look, a terrible flash, a deep broken sadness, and with that, he turned in the water and swam across to the other side. He was a good swimmer, bigger and stronger than the other kids. His uncle had a pool, so he swam often. Within a short time, he was sitting on the other bank. But he didn't say a word, just sat and stared off into the river.

Ava called to him, "Brett, please come back! I'm sorry I said that. Please, come back, this is so scary! Let's go home! I want to go home!"

Brett just sat and stared, the look of someone no longer there, the long stare. He was not hearing, he was not seeing, he was in some other place.

A kookaburra started to laugh, maybe even to mock, first slowly, but then relentless.

Brett looked up at him and started yelling, "Stop laughing at me! Shut up, shut up, just shut up!"

He leapt into the river and started his way back across. The kookaburra was joined by two more, and as Brett dog paddled, he yelled at them to stop one last time. Then all the splashing and movement ended as he dove under the water and was gone.

Vanished

The girls stood like stone statues, terrified, looking on, disbelieving, hoping he would pop up one more time and yell like he so often did. But he did not come up, not after a minute, or two or three or ten. He never came up.

They cried, they called to him, they sobbed deep tears, sadness upon the sadness of a life that was already so sad. They do not remember how long they stayed and looked up and down the river, praying, pleading, hoping to find him, and he never came.

The days and weeks that followed were full of sadness and despair. At first, the girls thought they should not tell, pretend they did not know what happened. They were ashamed they did not dive in to try and find Brett.

The adults came to the place, first a few, then many. Then divers and men and women with hooks and nets and machines to lift out the old trees from the river bed. This went on for days and more days and still Brett was never found. The girls were interviewed over and over again by parents, teachers, by police, but mostly by the other kids.

The adults were mostly kind as they tried to understand what happened, exactly where it happened. But the kids were relentless, and then the stories started.

No one knows where or how the story started, but it grew and took shape and meaning until it was irresistible, delicious, first to the children, then to the adults. These girls must have killed Brett, must have hidden the body. Why else could he not be found? These sweet girls were not at all sweet, they were something else. These girls were murders, nothing more, nothing less. These cousins that lived in the house that nobody ever visited and no one ever saw inside. They were not as they seemed. Brett was gone and never found, and they were with him. These girls were murderers.

* * *

"Ivy, everyone hates us," Ava spoke in a whisper in the lunch area outside the school principal's office. The school was located in the town of just 150 people, but it was a "central school" where kids were bussed from across the surrounding country. Years before, the tiny one-room schools in the area had closed, and someone, somewhere, decided a larger central school would be the best place for kids that lived far from any real civilized society.

"I don't think they hate us, I think they are scared of us now," Ivy responded in an even lower tone. Ivy was dark-haired and darker skinned than Ava, and together they made a striking pair. "I think they really think we killed Brett. They think we carried him off somewhere.

How could we? He was so much bigger than us! Why would we kill him, he was our best friend!"

Ivy sobbed but not with tears, and it was a silent crying, perhaps the worst kind. Just a slight heaving of her chest as she put her head on her knees.

Ava pulled her close, slowly, underneath the lunch bench so no one could see, and she too cried, a silent cry.

As days turned to a week and weeks to months, the story of Brett's disappearance did not diffuse, did not dissipate. It only grew and grew. Somehow, the big-city newspapers took hold of it and it started to spread throughout the state and then the country. More men came, bigger machines came, more dredging happened.

One day, when it looked like, finally, everyone was done with this story and moving onto the next, it happened.

Near the bank of the river, a tree had recently fallen and the earth turned up. A dog brought in to help with the search was walking back and forth around the base of the tree. It caught the eye of the trainer and he came over to see what the dog was so interested in. At first, there was nothing, but after some digging, they found it. First, a leg bone then a hand. The dog's owner cried out to a group of men by the river that he had found a body and they came running.

Murderers.

To tell of all the commotion that happened next would take far too long in this story, but indeed, they found a body. Many more people from the city came, everyone convinced it was Brett, somehow buried by two young girls at the base of an old tree.

In the end, it was not Brett but an elderly man, maybe eighty years old, they thought, probably white, and without any identity they could find. This was the time before DNA testing and the modern science of forensics, but it was declared to be an old man from long ago who had died or been buried by the banks of an ancient river many years before.

Brett was still gone, the girls still suspect, and now, another mystery had been laid upon the story.

Here, in this little town, a boy had gone missing, maybe killed by his classmates, and a mysterious old man found dead by the river. It was all too much, all too exciting, in this place near nowhere. So much excitement, so much cruelty to be done.

Brett

At first, the girls thought finding the old man's body by the tree where Brett disappeared would be a great distraction, a new twist that would deflect the cruel attention they got every day from the kids at school. It did not, it only added to the excitement, the tension, and the fear.

To Ava and Ivy, grieving the loss of their friend, the false hope only added to their misery. Brett had been a part of the girls' life from as far back as their memory could piece. He lived next door, visited them every day down by the river, and had been with them since kindergarten in the Central School. Brett was always there with them, taking on the role of protector and loving tormentor. They felt safe together.

He was the one Ava and Ivy could go to when they needed to complain or make fun of each other. If Ava and Ivy were bonded together for life, Brett was part of that glue, part of the substance that made the bond strong and hold through all the trials they had already lived through.

Ivy remembered a time when one of the boys in first grade pulled her off the monkey bars and she broke her arm. Brett was there in an instant, holding her arm and walking her to the teacher's office. Even at six years old, he comforted her and told her just how well broken arms healed, as he had done it twice when falling out of trees on the farm.

When Ivy returned to school the next day in a nice shiny cast, there was Brett again, the first to greet her—and with a new "friend." It was the boy that had made her fall. With his head down and in a tiny voice, he said sorry to Ivy. As Ivy accepted his apology in her own tiny voice, Brett led the contrite boy away. He spoke with the boy whom he towered over in height and looked back over his shoulder at Ivy with a curious smile that Ivy had never forgotten.

Even at that tender age she knew that this boy Brett was different, that this boy would always look after her. There was something different about him, something about the way he talked to her and looked at her that made her feel safe.

Every day after school the three would meet by the river. It never occurred to them they were too young to be roaming a giant farm down by a dangerous river in a land full of poisonous snakes and spiders. It is just what they did, what they had always done.

Brett rarely spoke about his home, but over the years the girls had put it together, mostly. Brett's mother died when he was born; she died as he was born, because he was born. His father never forgave him, nor did his brothers, despite his obvious innocence. Brett stayed away from the house on the bend in the river on their hill because he did not feel happy in that home. His father had barely spoken to him, or anyone, since his mother died.

They called his father "Silent Ted" at school. People made fun of Brett and his father that never spoke. Silent Ted was the butt of so many jokes at Brett's expense, he got sick of it and even, at times, fought the kids that mocked him. Never Ava and Ivy, though, which was part of the reason he spent all his time with them. They would tease each other as kids so love to do, but these two knew the things that really hurt Brett deep in his heart; his father, the silent father, was one of them.

One day the girls found Brett sitting under a tree at the turn in the river, his favorite place. He sat quietly crying as they sat down next to him. He never looked up.

"I wish I had died, not my mum," he said. "My dad never talks to me. He thinks I killed her and he never talks to me. He just looks at me with his mean eyes whenever I say anything." He cried between the words. "I don't want to go home! He hates me and I didn't even do anything!" The crying turned to deep heavy sobs.

The girls did not know what to say, so they said nothing. They simply sat with Brett and put their arm around him and stayed until the crying stopped. They did not know that this was exactly what he needed, perhaps even he did not know it, but in that simple act, they knew Brett felt not so alone, not so sad. They knew he felt like he had a family on the river, even though he did not have one in his house.

Brett had dreams, lots of dreams. He dreamed of far-off places and adventures, and in those dreams the girls would always be with him. One dream he kept having he told no one about it, but kept it to himself. He dreamed of a faraway place where he would have to do a very brave thing to save the one he loved. He did not know exactly what love was, but he knew that he loved this one and he would always protect her.

He worried about the dream because he did not feel like a brave person. He wondered if any kid actually felt brave, which seemed like a thing that only adults could be. So, he worried that when the time came in that far-off place, maybe he would not be brave, maybe he would not do what needed to be done to save the one he loved. He worried that in that moment he would regret it for the rest of his life. Being brave seemed like such a big thing, he kept having the dream and kept wondering how it was to be brave.

Brett thought many times that it was a curious thing to live on a farm next to another farm, next to two girls his age that also did not like to go home. He did not take it for granted that the very people that could save him from a very sad life lived right next door. Not his actual life, but the feelings that go with a life. It turns out that a few close friends can change a life, can make a life worthy of the living of it, and without them, it would be too sad to go on.

Even though "next door" was a few miles away, it was still very close. He knew many other kids at his school, but none of them lived in a magical place like he did. This place with all its animals only found in Australia. This place where the night was so dark the entire universe could open up over your head. This place with a river that flowed and gave a strip of green life in an otherwise dry and foreboding landscape. This place that one could roam for hours and never go over the same ground again. This place that men from the time before had lived for tens of thousands of years.

It seemed everything about this place was magical, not least the girls on the farm next door. He even wondered what he would choose if he were given the choice. If he could get back his family but have to give up this place and the girls, which would he choose? It was a terrible thought but it would keep coming up. What a terrible choice, a family you never had or the people you had that were, in the end, your other family.

The more he tried to stop thinking about it, the more it came over him. This was the thing with sad or scary thoughts, the more you tried to stop them, the more they came. So, he learned a trick: he imagined that in some magical place he could have both. A mother and father that loved him, and still live on the farm near the girls. This was a most excellent thought and a most excellent dream to have.

It was in this place, in his mind, that he went when he was alone down by the river at the bend under that tree. When he went to that place in his mind, he thought that indeed he could be brave enough to do the hard thing that he was sure would come.

THE TORTURE

I t has been said that kids are the most tortuous, the worst terrorists, the most brazen and cruel of us all. Childhood is perhaps the time when we are the most insecure, the most frightened, and the most likely to form a clan.

Ava and Ivy were now outcasts. No one, at least in public, would speak to them in anything but mocking terms. "Ava and Ivy, they are gay, they took young Brett's life away!" was a favorite little ditty.

At first the girls did not know what it meant. Their confusion was quickly fixed by another boy in class who announced their obvious orientation and love for each other in the cruelest of poems. Whoever said, "sticks and stones may break my bones, but words will never hurt me" did not know these words. Whoever came up with that saying had never been a middle school kid on the outside of the "in" tribe.

Sticks and stones *were* thrown at them. Heads slapped, shins kicked, but the words were worse. Ava had to see the school nurse for a deep cut over her eye when an actual stone cracked her head and she bled all over her face. But none of it was as bad as the teasing. None of it compared to the shame and sadness of the rhymes and relentless mocking.

A favorite game was for someone to run by and touch them and scream with delight, "Ava and Ivy germs!" as they held their fingers high and ran after the other kids to transfer the pestilence. The caught kid would then run to the next victim screaming the same retort, "Av and Ivy germs!" and when they tagged the next kid, scream with delight, "Tag! You're it, you got the germs!"

It was relentless, these games, the teasing, it never stopped. In class, it was tolerable, as the teachers mostly tried to put a cap on it. But every break, every snack time, lunch time, before and after school time, the harassment was constant.

The bus ride home was the worst. Ava and Ivy lived three miles from town down a dusty road, and every day they took the school bus with thirty or forty other kids who were also dropped off along that road at their stops. This was common in those days, many kids had to walk another mile or more from the bus stop to their homes on the farms that lined those dusty trails. The bus ride was the perfect place to torture the outcasts. It was a locked room on wheels, a prison yard for the girls for forty-five minutes a day, both ways.

The morning bus ride was tolerable. The kids were tired and being cruel takes energy. The bus ride home, though, was terrifying. All those kids, ramped up from being locked in class all day, finally free, school out, bus ride home, victims to victimize, bus driver unaware or too tired to care. Physical fights were common, verbal abuse a constant.

Worst of all, the kids were not just from their class but all the way to year twelve, seniors in high school. Just when you think a thirteen-year-old could not be crueler, watch how they act when they want to impress a senior in high school. They went to another level, and with great delight, the high-school kids joined in and added an extra level of sick sophistication to the game.

Ava and Ivy fought back at first. They protested, spat back, punched back, yelled back, but it became too much, too relentless. So, like a defeated army, they retreated. They sat together, heads down, hands held, tears held in as best they could. Tears to these kids was like blood to a vampire, seeing them would bring on a new level of cruelty. Keeping the tears in was the girls' number-one goal. Seeing them holding hands brought on the old favorite, "Ava and Ivy, they are gay, they took young Brett's life away!" But they would not let even this stop them from holding onto each other. It was all they had, without each other they had nothing.

When, finally, the bus reached their gate, they would jump off and run, because most of the time a can, a bottle, a stick would be thrown in their direction, rarely hitting but always threatening. When the bus drove off and they were free, they would drop to their knees and cry together.

On this day, Ava was first to gather her strength. "I am not going back, Ivy, I cannot take it anymore," she said with complete resolve.

"What will you do, where will you go?" Ivy asked, already convinced Ava was not bluffing. Ivy felt the same but saw no way out.

"I don't know, maybe I can pretend to go to school and then just go to the river and spend the day there and come home at the end of the day," Ava mused.

"The teachers will tell on you. They will tell Mum and they will find you and make you go back," Ivy declared.

"Mum doesn't care, she doesn't even know where we are most of the time," Ava said sadly.

"Then they will take you to another school with nuns and priests and lock you in your room. I heard one of the big boys talking about it," Ivy said. "He said we should be 'instituted' or something, like jail for kids." Ivy started to cry again.

"I am not going to any kids' jail!" Ava almost yelled. "I'll run away, I'll hide, they'll never find me, never!"

They both sat crying a little, but mostly just sat and stared. It was all too much. They had done nothing wrong and yet there was all this. The one thing they had outside each other and their farm was school and their friends, and now that was gone. And not just gone, but now a place they hated, feared, a place they could not return to.

Running away seemed like the only plan, but that seemed so very frightening. They were only thirteen, but they had heard the stories on the bus of what happened to young girls that ran away. The things that happened to them, terrible things, if they were caught by those kinds of men. They could never be caught, they had to never be caught by those kinds of people.

So, their fear grew and their sadness with it.

THE

LONG WALK

Wiping their tears away, the girls decided to take a long walk home, a *really* long walk home, across the paddocks, down to the river. On the way, they played their usual games. One of their favorites was to chase the mice that lived underground and could be summoned by beating the ground, or even better, pouring water down one hole and having them run out of another connected hole. In the past, they would join their brothers and take up a stick and try to squash the mice.

There were years when the mice came in plagues. So many mice, so much destruction, the farmers and adults encouraged the practice of killing the mice but it was futile. During those plagues, the mice were like soldiers from an overwhelming invading army, so many they could never be stopped.

One day, walking from school, Ivy looked up and asked if someone had painted the white grain silo brown. The shed was at least fifty feet high and thirty feet around and was, until today, a bright white. Now it was brown. It wasn't until they got close that they realized, to their horror, what was happening.

The entire side of the silo was covered in mice, one on another, making a ladder to the top where they were jumping into the silo and feasting on the grain below. It was terrifying and yet they could not look away. They pulled out their sticks and started to hit at the mice, thousands and thousands of them, but for every one they felled, ten more would join. They felt something between rage, fear, and exhalation. Girl against nature.

These mice did not just head to the grain silos during these times, they were everywhere. In the house, in the kitchen, in your bed at night, in your clothes. Ivy's mother said when Ivy was born there were mice in the bed with her in the hospital. Farmers often broke down and cried, as a year's worth of work could be eaten by these crazed mice in just a few days. Despite all the work they did sealing the silos, they always found a way in, a way to turn a poor farmer into a destitute one.

Two years earlier, they had come across a man sitting on a kitchen chair out in a paddock by his grain silo. He was sitting very quietly drinking from a bottle and just watching silently. They knew that silent sad cry. Mice were all over the ground, the silo, and some were even crawling on him. He seemed not to notice or to care.

The girls ran off, scared to see such sadness, so much giving up. They headed to the river, to their safe place, and in the distance from where they had come, they heard a sound, like the crack of a tree branch only louder. They knew what it was, they were country girls. It took only a brief glance at each other to confirm the noise was not in their heads. They never again spoke of it again.

Today the plague was over but some mice always remained. They played their game of rooting out the mice and chasing them, but they had lost the desire to kill them. It seemed cruel, pointless. They had their little mouse families and were just trying to live like everything else on this harsh land.

Yet they still enjoyed chasing them and squealing and laughing. They thought maybe the mice liked it, too, or at least that is what they told themselves. When it got really hot, they could not find any, and they thought maybe the mice went down as low as they could to get cool, and not even their loudest noises and beating could make them come out. The mice were safe, safe from everything above, from the girls and anything else that might want to catch them.

"I wish I could go down that hole with them," Ava sighed. "Right down that hole and maybe turn into a mouse and live a little mouse life away from up here."

"I could come with you and we would be mouse friends and burrow holes all the way to the river and no one could find us or tease us ever again," Ivy chimed in. "I would miss my bike though," she giggled.

"Maybe we could make a really tiny one for you to ride through the tunnels like a little circus mouse," Ava added.

Something about that image broke the girls up. First a few giggles, then they were laughing so hard it hurt, the tears streaming down their faces, dirt and sand making little rivers on their cheeks. Then the crying became sad and they hugged each other as the weight of the thing swept over them.

After a time, they found a tree and slept a restless, exhausted sleep in the shade. They were so very tired. Not from the walk but from the weight of being so sad over losing Brett and so outcast from the kids at school.

Then the dreams came, strange dreams of a far-off place, of people and things they knew but could not quite understand. In Ava's dream, there was a figure in the distance, a small man, perhaps, or a large boy. He was gesturing for Ava to come over, to follow him. She woke up with a fright, a giant ant on her leg that had taken a nip to see what she tasted like.

When Ivy woke, Ava was gone. She looked all around but could not see her anywhere. It seemed like it was still the same time of day, she had not slept that long, she was sure. She started to panic.

"Ava, Ava, where are you?" she cried.

At first, there was nothing, just a kookaburra in a tree nearby that started to laugh, slowly at first but then faster and faster.

"Ava, *Aaaaa-vaaaa!*" Ivy cried.

From behind a tree about a hundred yards away, Ava emerged, pulling up her pants and walking toward Ivy. "I'm here! I just had to pee, stop freaking out!" she yelled.

As Ava got closer, she stared over Ivy's head in a quizzical look she got sometimes when she did not know what she was looking at, or knew exactly what she was looking at but was lost in far-off thoughts.

Ivy turned around and looked up and saw what had caught Ava's attention. They had walked so far they were all the way to the ring tree. They had slept beneath its branches, had dreamed under its shade. With all their talking and mouse jokes, they had not noticed just how far they had come. How could they have missed seeing the tree? It was a local legend.

"Wow!" Ivy exclaimed. "We walked a long way, no wonder we fell asleep."

The ring tree was on the far corner of their property, miles and miles from the houses on the hill. They could not remember ever actually walking to it before. It was a marker they used near the road to tell when they were close to home, but always from a car seat or a bus as they drove by, kicking up the red dirt.

The ring tree was not only a sign they were home, it was a local attraction, a big gum tree whose largest branches had been fashioned into a ring by the people who lived here in times past. The ones who had lived here so long no one was exactly sure just how long it was. They had mostly gone now as the new people, the pale people, Ava and Ivy's people, had come. Yet this tree remained.

It was wonderful and mysterious, and even the big boys who liked to shoot and burn and break everything did not touch it. In this place, this tree was special. Everyone that saw it could see and even feel this tree was from another time, another place, the time before the time of these new people.

Ava and Ivy stared up at the big ring and saw a crow sitting on a lower branch, just staring at them. Seemingly not bothered in the slightest by their presence, just staring with its head to the side as crows do, looking, wondering. Its black, sheer feathers in stark contrast to the impossibly blue sky behind it.

"It's staring at us, Ava!" Ivy said with surprise. "Like, really staring at us."

"Maybe it was watching me pee!" Ava giggled and Ivy laughed.

"Well, peeing is a funny thing, but pooping out here is gross and no one wants to see that!" Ivy said. "Do you think crows poop while they fly and try to hit people they don't like?" she asked in a somewhat serious manner.

"I don't know," Ava mused. "But if I were a crow, I would poop-dive just about every kid at school and cover them from head to toe! And I'd do it every day!" With that, she fell to her knees and started laughing at the thought of it.

Since Brett died, the girls did this a lot, travel from hysterics to crying in a moment's notice. It was like there was this giant well of emotion inside them, and when they let a little crack open, all the feelings would flow out. Sometimes it was laughter and sometimes it was tears. Sometimes they looked at each other during these times and knew something was not right with them. They were too full of these emotions, too ready to explode.

Sometimes they would start laughing or crying without any provocation, for no reason. When that happened, the other knew where it came from, they knew the place, the furnace that created the magma that could start flowing at any time. They knew it because it lived in them, it flowed in them, it bonded them. They shared the same magma, they feared it, even though it was part of them. It was the pain of a lost mother, a lost dearest friend, the rejection of kids turned against them at school, and the general feeling that despite the beauty of this place, their lives were somehow broken.

"Want to try and climb into the ring?" Ava challenged. The ring of the tree was big enough to easily sit three adults, let alone two young girls. The trick was to get up to it as it was at least ten feet off the ground.

"Do you think we should?" Ivy questioned, looking up at it. "Almost no one ever does. Brett tried once and his dad hit him and screamed at him to never climb this tree. At least, that's what he told me."

"I know, I heard one of the teachers say it should be protected and that no one should even touch it. She said it's been here for hundreds of years and if kids get too close they might wreck it by carving their names into it and peeing on it," Ava recounted. "But I think it's okay to try. We're not very big and we would never hurt it. And it would be such a fun thing to do!"

"How do we get up there? It's way taller than us and there's no way we could boost each other up that high," Ivy said sadly.

"I have an idea!" Ava blurted out. "I got it while I was peeing—I get a lot of ideas while I am having a wiz!" She giggled. "Under the trees are these great sticks and all this long sticky bark that comes off like strips. I bet we could make a ladder out of them and climb up! I saw my brother do it once and it worked pretty well for a while. Well, until it broke and he busted his head," she laughed. "We weigh a lot less, I bet it could hold us really well. Let's try it!"

With that, they began gathering the right sized sticks and lots of the stringy bark from the gum trees. You had to use the new bark, the old bark was too dry and just broke. Just like her brother had done, Ava tied the sticks together and wrapped the bark around the ends of the sticks, fashioning what looked, if you looked hard, a ladder.

"It looks like a Dr. Seuss ladder to me," Ivy noted. "All crazy and weird-looking, but kind of like a ladder."

After about an hour of toil, they lifted the ladder and put it up against the tree. It was too short, but close enough that Ava thought she could scramble up the last part using a big knot with a hole in it on the lowest side of the ring.

"You stand here and hold it while I try to climb up," Ava declared. "And catch me if it breaks!"

"There is no way I am catching you if you fall, you'll squash me!" Ivy declared. "Let's make a bed out of the bark to break your fall if you slip or it breaks," she suggested.

So, they gathered up a big pile of bark and made a landing pad should Ava fall from the ladder.

Ivy tested it by taking a running jump and landing square in the middle. She let out a big "Ooof!" as she rolled off. "Well, it ain't no mattress, but it's better than nothing."

Ava stared up the ladder. As soon as she took her first step, the kookaburras started to laugh, first one then others chimed in.

"Seems like they think you're going to fall, Ava, and they're getting ready to pee themselves when you do!" Ivy exclaimed.

Ava went up another rung, slowly, cautiously, as the birds got louder.

"Wow, they really are excited for you!" Ivy called up.

Another rung, then another. One kookaburra even flew to the tree and onto the ring and stared down at Ava. The laughter of the birds was really picking up, as if they could tell how exciting this all was and how potentially dangerous if Ava actually fell.

Ava took another step and the rung broke, but she instinctively grabbed the next rung up and held on. The kookaburras were really laughing now, apparently loving this entertainment. Two birds on the ring looked at her now, standing side by side as if judging her performance.

"You okay, Ava? Let's stop now, come down! I'm worried you're going to fall and we're so far from home!" Ivy called up.

"I'm okay! I'm almost there. I can already see over to the river, it's amazing! I can see the bend and the old shed on the other side," Ava declared, and took hold of the next rung on the ladder.

Now she was at the top of the ladder, maybe ten feet up, way over Ivy's head. This was the tricky part. She had to reach over to get her foot into the hole in the knot of the tree and push herself up. She loved gymnastics during PE at school, so stretching out was pretty easy, but pushing up was going to be the hard part, as she still had tiny, skinny "spindle legs" Ivy's brother told her.

She decided to do it in one motion, lean over to her right, jam her foot into the hole, then jump right up onto the lower branch of the ring tree.

Ava was so focused on her next move she did not notice what was happening around her. The kookaburras were now in a frenzy, crying and laughing in a maniacal manner. A bunch of crows had come to see what all the racket was about and a mob of kangaroos in the distance had stopped and were staring in their direction, seemingly transfixed by the sight of a girl climbing up a tree.

Ivy saw all of this and called out to Ava. "Come down, I have a bad feeling! The animals are going crazy and they're scaring me. Please come down, let's go home!" She was too shaken to cry but she wanted to.

"I'm so close! I am not coming down! If I make it up here, you can follow and maybe we never have to come down, we can live in this tree!" Ava announced.

Ivy pleaded with her. "Please, Ava, please, I'm so scared! This was a bad idea, you might get hurt and we're really far from home!"

The birds seemed to agree and their laughter got even louder.

Ava was determined, and without another thought, she stretched out her leg, found the hole with her foot, and pushed up with all her might.

She had underestimated her strength. With her foot firmly in the hole by the knot, she pushed hard and up and landed on the branch belly-first, almost slipping right off the other side. She steadied herself and got to a sitting position.

The laughter started to settle as Ivy called up to her, "Are you okay? What can you see? I think I peed my pants a little!" She laughed.

There was no reply, Ava had sat up and was staring into the distance.

"What do you see?" Ivy called out, looking up at her friend.

Ava just sat staring out into the distance with a far-off look that Ivy had seen before. Then she started to stand up.

"Ava, sit down, you're going to fall! Please, sit down! You're so high up!" Ivy called out in panic.

Again, Ava did not respond, she just looked out into the distance with a blank look, not one of fear but more of wonder. Finally, she looked down at Ivy. "Ivy, I'm going now. You should come," she said softly.

The kookaburra on the tree next to her looked out in the same direction as Ava, then back to Ava again.

"What are you talking—"

But before Ivy could finish, Ava spread her arms and leaned forward like in a swan dive and fell forward.

Ivy panicked. She was falling on the wrong side of the tree, there was no mattress of bark and sticks to break her fall!

Then she was gone.

Ivy fell back, at first confused then frightened, terrified. Ava had disappeared, gone. Ivy got up and looked up in the tree again then all around. She must have blinked, missed Ava's fall. But she was gone, just gone.

Terrified, Ivy called out to her. What was happening? She must still be asleep, but she did not feel asleep, she knew she wasn't asleep. She kept looking for Ava and calling her name and finally fell to the ground and curled into a ball in the dirt and wept tears of sadness and fear.

She could not decide if she was going mad or if what she had seen was real, but she did know Ava was not with her and that was the worst part. That was the part that would break her. She could not stay in this place without Ava, she was sure of it.

THE LOST GIRL

Ivy woke to the cry of her mother. "She's gone! Oh my God, she's gone!" She burst into Ivy's room, yelling, "Where is she? Where's Ava? I had a dream that she ran away and was in danger and now she's gone. Ivy, where is she?"

Ivy sat straight up in bed. Confused, sore all over. What happened, was it real?

Her mother looked at her. "Oh my God, what happened to you, Ivy?" she cried, dumbfounded.

Ivy looked down and saw blood on her sheets, her t-shirt was torn and dirt covered her arms and legs. She could not see properly so she rubbed her eyes and face and found more dried blood caked on her face.

"I don't know," Ivy responded. "I don't know!" She started to cry.

"Stop crying! Where is Ava? What happened, what have you done?" Her mother was yelling in that slurred voice Ivy now recognized as a permanent fixture in her mother's life. The slur of one too many chardonnays, first at night, then in the afternoon, then lunch, now all day.

"I don't know! We were at the ring tree and she disappeared. I ran home, but I can't remember getting home. I don't know where Ava is!" She shivered a deep cold shiver from her bones and cried even more. Tears of loss and fear and sadness took over her.

"What are you talking about, Ivy? The ring tree is miles from here! What have you done? Where did all that blood come from? What have you done, Ivy!" Her mother's voice had now turned accusing.

"I didn't do anything! Ava just disappeared."

It was at that moment she realized this was not a dream, this was very real. Ava had gone, but how? It must be a dream, but no. Ivy had dreams all the time, some good, some terrifying, but they were nothing like this. This was the real world, she had watched Ava disappear.

Even as she thought it, she knew one thing very clearly: no one would believe her. How could they? People don't disappear like that, that is not a thing. Kids disappear in a river, that might happen, but kids don't disappear in plain sight.

Ivy looked up and her mother was gone. She heard her in the next room, on the phone, and she could not make out what was being said but she was talking fast and dropping the "F" word a lot.

Ivy's mother burst back into the room and yelled, "I called the cops, so you better start talking! What have you done?"

"I didn't do anything, Mum! Ava disappeared from the ring tree, she just fell and never landed," Ivy pleaded for her mother to believe her.

"What are you talking about? Have you gone crazy or something? First Brett, then the dead guy, now Ava? What the hell have you done?" Her mother was screaming now, a terrifying drunken rant that Ivy knew all too well.

At that moment, Ivy knew what she had to do. She had to run. In an instant, she played out what would happen next. The cops would come, she would tell her story, they would think she was crazy, or worse, some kind of a serial killer, and she would be sent away to a home, a jail, some jail-home for kids, and never be seen again. She flashed back to Ava's face and her last words. "You should come, Ivy."

And with that, Ivy darted for the door.

Ivy's mother tried to grab her, but she was too drunk to make the move and fell over a table next to the door. She cried out to Ivy to stop, but Ivy didn't slow down, not even for a second.

She ran out the front door and onto her bicycle, then headed down the dirt path to the paddock below, peddling as fast as she could. She was headed to the ring tree, but this time she would go via the river. Down by the river, over the years, the girls had worn a bike track. Usually, they walked and explored, but other days they took their bikes.

This day she had to ride faster and longer than she ever had. She had to get to the tree before the people came. She knew *all* the people would be coming. All the cops, all the farmers, and then all the kids, everyone would be coming for her for the rest of her life. She had to get away, she had to go fast.

The good thing about living on this farm was that the closest police station was at least twenty miles away and it would take them at least an hour to get here by the time they got the call. The bad news was that the cops all grew up here and knew the roads and the farms really well.

Ivy realized that even though her mother was drunk, she would remember that she said Ava disappeared at the ring tree and they would be headed there at some point. Ivy figured she had little time to make it to the tree, but even as she raced to her destination, she did not know what she would do when she got there.

She slowed her pace as the thoughts started to take hold. *If they think I killed Ava and find me at the tree, they will take me away. If I hide and run away, maybe I have a chance, maybe they will not find me.* But where to hide? And for how long? When would they stop looking for her? She had an idea. She stopped her bike, jumped off, and pushed it into the river.

Once the bike disappeared under the water, she ran farther up to the bend in the river the locals called Norah's

Bend. Ivy's brother had said Norah was a prostitute that lived there a hundred years ago, back when the paddle steamers went up and down the river with their goods and cargo. Norah "serviced" the workers as they passed and she was quite the local legend. So famous they named the bend in the river after her.

No one knows where she went, but one day she just disappeared. The stories were that she was a great beauty and no one could understand why she chose this line of work. A woman like that could find her way into all kinds of places in society, but here she was in the bend of a river miles from any town, doing the work that Ivy could not really understand. It was just about the grossest thing she could think of. Yet this was the place.

While no one had seen Norah in a century, her old shack still remained. No one ever went there, it was small, broken-down, and the kids in the area said it was haunted. The most frightening story was that Norah had gotten into a fight with one of the sailors and she had been killed right there in the shack. Her ghost roamed the banks, and apparently, she was particularly fond of children. It is why so many children died in the river, they supposed. Norah's ghost would come and swim up the river and drown them in all her ghostly rage and sadness.

Ivy did not believe in ghosts. There were lots of things in this world to be afraid of but ghosts were not one of them for her. Terrified of the water as she was, she made her plan.

A hundred yards past the bend in the river was an old tree that had fallen down and lay almost halfway across the river. One reason the steamers stopped traveling this river was these trees would fall and partially sink and the boats would often crash into them. This was a big river but it was no Mississippi, her geography teacher had told them. On this river, fallen trees were always a threat even to the most experienced captain. So when the roads came, the steamers left.

To the kids on the river, though, these fallen trees were a constant source of excitement. A fallen tree, especially one that had not sunk all the way into the river, was a delight. The bravest kids would walk out on the tree into the river as far as they dared while the other kids held their breath. The kids knew that these trees, as big as they were, could move and sink at any time and take a kid with them.

There were many stories over the years of kids playing this game and never coming back up. Brett was gone, but he was not the first. Though every time a kid was lost, the game seemed more and more dangerous and the kids played it less and less.

Today, for Ivy, this was no game, she had a plan. She looked around and found an old hollowed-out branch about her height. She was going to walk out on that fallen tree right to the end and then with her branch held tight, jump into the water and kick paddle her way to the other bank.

This all sounded like a great plan until she reached the fallen tree and her gut went into a spasm. It hurt so bad she had to go do her business in the bushes immediately. This sometimes happened when she was extra scared, the need to go could not be stopped. She ran behind a tree and squatted, then cleaned up as best she could, with a series of leaves and sticks and a hand wash in the river. It was gross but it was a thing all the country kids did and with practice it could turn out pretty well. One of the old jokes the boys loved went something like, "How do you keep Ozzy flies off your face? Go poop in the paddock," or something like that.

It was while she was squatting behind the tree that she saw them. Off in the distance but headed her way were two motor bikes and a four-wheel drive. She got lower and thanked the need to go that she was not standing upright on the river bed or they would have seen her. She giggled about thanking her bowels, but that only lasted a second. She had to run!

Ivy returned to the fallen tree in a ninja-like move, and while no longer in pain, she was no less scared. In the distance, she could hear motorcycles getting closer. Motor bikes were one of the preferred modes of transport for the farmers as they could get into places even the four-wheel drives could not. She had to move fast or they would find her.

She started across the branch, moist, slippery and worst of all, wobbly. Each step the tree moved, up and down, partially floating on the water and also moving side to side. She got on all threes, as her fourth limb, her right arm, clutched the hollow branch. She inched across the fallen tree as fast as she could without slipping off as the sound of the motorcycles grew louder. They were coming toward her, she was sure. Or were they going past her to the ring tree? She could not tell, but she had to go faster. She pressed on, ever faster, ever lower to keep her balance, her face right on the tree trunk now.

Then she saw it, not two feet away!

Like an apparition, it lay staring at her. Eyes trained on her, those slaty backward eyes so dark, so sinister. She gave out an audible squeak even as she tried to keep holding onto the log, then recoiled and almost slipped into the water. Here in front of her was one of nature's most frightening animals, at least to her. A brown snake sunned itself on a log in the river, minding its own business but able to kill a girl her size in short order.

All the kids know about this snake, about all the snakes in this area. The rule was easy: if you see a snake, it is almost certainly one of the most poisonous in the world, and if you get properly bitten, you would die before any help could arrive. The kids had this drilled into them every day, every night, all the time. Snakes were killers, stay away.

The good news was most of them did not want anything to do with people, and given the chance, they would back up and take off. If they were cornered, though, they would strike, and they were fast, so very fast.

Her uncle was a snake handler and would come to school and show off the snakes he had caught at people's homes, on their porch, in their bedrooms, even in the school cafeteria. He would grab them by the tail and when the snake tried to rise up and bite him, he would twist their bodies the other way and they would have to start their rise again. He kept doing it until they gave up to catch their breath before starting again.

The kids and teachers were awestruck and terrified. He had been bitten before and even spent a week in the hospital, and he told the kids over and over again, "If you see a snake, just get the hell out of its way!"

Ivy could not get out of this guy's way. He was between her and hope. Between her and escape. She had never been more terrified, but without even thinking, in one quick movement, she took her hollow branch and swiped at the snake. She missed and the snake now was pissed. It hissed at her and started to rear up and the back of its body started to coil, ready to strike. It had not started this fight but it was determined to win it.

For a moment, Ivy thought about jumping in the water and swimming back to shore—better the guys on the bikes than this slimy friend. But the thought of what might happen if she did that was too much, so she swung the branch like a cricket bat and hit the snake, now a foot above the tree, under the head. It was just enough to make even this sure-bellied snake slip a little, then a little more, then a lot as it struggled to stay on the fallen tree. Try as it might, it fell into the river and for a second disappeared.

There was no relief for Ivy, for as soon as it disappeared, it reappeared on the top of the water. But to Ivy's eternal thanks, it was headed away from the tree, now wanting no part of this fight. It did turn for a moment and look back at Ivy, giving her a curious snake look, probably making sure the attacker was not following. To Ivy, though, it seemed like it was warning her: stay away from this place, this is a dangerous place, not a place for little girls. Then off it went right across the water, out of sight.

For a moment, Ivy sat, or rather sprawled, catching her breath, shivering even though the day was hot and the sun was already peaking. Then she heard the sound of the bikes again and it shocked her into movement. She crawled on, this time looking up with every move to make sure Mr. Snake had no family members sunning themselves awake this fine morning.

She reached the end of the tree and now it was time to take the plunge. She guessed the other bank was maybe one hundred feet away, but she knew she could make it. She had her log, and years of experience throwing the same kind of logs in the river had taught her how well they floated. This was not the thought that carried her. It was Brett and the stories of other kids that had drowned in this river.

As she inched to the edge, she saw his face, just like it had been when he dived into the river that one last time.

Her friend, all the way back to kindergarten. The boy she saw almost every day by this river. That sad face, then the terror of him never coming back up. She missed that face, that boy. It was one of the first times she thought of him as a boy and not just as Brett. It was a curious feeling.

Yet she was so scared! Would she drown too? What would that feel like? Was there actually a ghost that dragged you down to the bottom of the river? Would that snake come back and bite her while she was flailing, and was it floating over the water's surface like some kind of an Olympic swimmer?

All she needed was the sound coming behind her, louder now. Without another thought, she slipped into the water and started kicking her feet as quickly and quietly as possible with the branch out in front of her.

One thing Ivy did not account for was the flow of the river. It looked so calm from the river bank, but just under the surface it was moving fast. At first, she started to panic, she was moving so quickly down the river, she would never make it across.

Then she remembered what a lifeguard had taught the kids one year when they went to the beach up near Melbourne, the big city many hours away. He talked about rip tides and how they could carry you away but the trick was not to fight them. The trick was to swim parallel to the "rip" and it would carry you down the beach, but eventually would let you go. If you tried to swim against it, even if you were a great swimmer, you would run out of energy before the ocean did and you would drown.

So Ivy just kept on kicking across the river, even as down the river she went. It was hard to see if she was getting closer, but after a while she could see the trees move clearly and knew she was making progress. Just as she thought she might be far enough across to put her feet down someone grabbed her and pulled her under the water.

At first, it was so shocking she was not even scared, just surprised that the guys on the bikes could have caught her so fast. Then she realized it was not a person but a thing and this thing was another sunken tree branch. It had caught her shirt as she floated by and, with the flowing current, had pulled her under the water.

She tried to reach back and untangle herself but she could not. Her shirt was now wrapped around the tree in a way she could not figure out in her now-increasing panic. She tried again to reach back but again could not get it free, and now in the struggle was needing desperately to come up for air. Her only hope was to get the shirt off, so she ripped at the buttons on the front and in a moment she was free.

Her head popped out of the water and she took a long huge gasp of air, then another. As soon as she felt better, she went straight to the mortifying thought that now she had no shirt, until she remembered she had on a t-shirt underneath and was relieved and surprised that one moment she thought she might die of drowning and the next might die of embarrassment. She was trying to decide which was worse when she got sucked down into the water again.

This time there was no tree, there was movement all around her, bubbles and noises and mud and that sucking pressure pulling her down. Confused about what was happening, she wondered if it was an earthquake. Not that she knew what that felt like, but she had seen the movies with all the people falling in the cracks of the earth never to be seen again. But they didn't have earthquakes here, so what was happening?

She struggled to swim up to the surface, but the water was all churned up and the pressure pulling her down continued. As she struggled, she remembered the teachers saying that the river had lots of erosion and small cave-ins that could collapse at any time, and as the bank fell into the water, it could drag the dirt, water, and any person standing there down with it. This must be what was happening. Maybe her pulling on that tree had made something give way and the river was settling back into place, with her soon to be part of the river floor.

She was out of breath now, her lungs screaming, and it was everything she could do to not take a breath. Then she saw Ava. She saw her in the distance, on the ring tree, only this time someone was standing with her. Ava's back was to her at first but she had turned her head and called for Ivy to come. Then the figures fell off the tree and once more disappeared.

Ivy scrambled one last time, but she could not make it to the surface. She tried to take in a breath, then everything went black.

Norah's House

The next sensation Ivy had was of coughing, lots of coughing, and a bright light, so bright she could not see. She was confused, where was she? She remembered being in the river, being pulled down, now she was coughing and not seeing because of a bright light. She had heard the last thing people see when they die was a light, so she must be dead.

She was on the river bank now, in the mud, but safely out of the water. Suddenly, she threw up all over herself, one big stream of vomit pouring out of her. She stopped with a heaving gasp of air then rolled over and vomited again. She hated vomiting, it felt so bad and you could not stop it.

She looked down at it, and as always, to her surprise, there they were—diced carrots. One of her brother's great revelations was that no matter what you had been eating, when you threw up there were always diced carrots in the puke. What was that? It was like your stomach was a diced carrot factory ready to produce the carrots whenever you blew chunks, and the chunks were always, of course, diced carrots.

The good news about vomiting all over herself and seeing the diced carrots was that it was evidence that she was not, in fact, dead. Never in her short life had she heard tales of vomiting your guts out in heaven. Surely, if this was a thing, people would have been talking about it for thousands of years. First a bright light, then you see Baby Jesus, then you vomit your guts out. No one would leave out that last bit, it was too interesting and gross, a highlight worth noting. No, she was sure now she was alive and the vomiting proved it.

The river must have carried her to its banks and delivered her on her back and she had survived, but not without taking in some huge swallows of river water, which would make even the toughest person vomit their head off.

Finally, the vomiting stopped but the coughing remained, like when you drink too fast and it goes down the wrong hole into your lungs. The lungs were trying to clear themselves but it was beginning to hurt. It was not stopping and nothing was coming up.

She had often wondered why the body did this, continuing with its ways long after it had done its job. She hit her thumb with a hammer once and screamed in pain. Ava was with her, as always, and through her tears she wondered why the pain kept going for so long. Ava tried to explain, as had been explained to her, that the pain was to protect you from injuring herself, but Ivy did not buy it.

"I already injured myself, why doesn't the pain stop now? I got it, don't hit your thumb with a hammer, so why won't it stop!" Ivy cried.

"I guess so you won't do it again. It's making sure you don't forget how painful hitting your thumb with a hammer is. You're not very bright, Ivy, so it has to make the lesson very clear," Ava joked and despite her pain, Ivy joined in with a mix of tears and laughter.

Thinking of it now, Ivy became very sad. She had known it her whole life, but right now she felt it like never before, she loved Ava so much. They were more than cousins; they were best friends, but even more than that. Through the life they led on this farm, with all the sadness in that house on the hill, all the loss that came from Brett's death and the kids at school tormenting them, they were bonded. They had become like one person. Losing Ava had been like losing her arms or legs or eyes, she was no longer whole.

She was too tired to cry so she just lay there, thinking about Ava and overwhelmed by the sadness and loss of it. Without Ava, she did not want to go on. She had kind of died when Ava disappeared, even though she kept running. This crazy idea of hiding and disappearing was not working out, and now she had just lost interest in the thing, in all of it. She wished the river had not delivered her back to the world. Right now, she wished it had just taken her down.

The sadness soon passed and it was replaced with courage. She had to get to the ring tree, to try and go where Ava had gone! If she got caught, if they took her away, she would escape and go back to the tree until it took her away. A life without Ava was no life. She would go find her or she would have no life.

But where Ava had gone, of course, was a question that would not stop going around and around in her head. It seemed to Ivy that Ava had been transported, like in one of those Sci-Fi movies, like the transporter in *Star Trek*. Here one moment, somewhere far off the next. She knew such things were supposed to be fantasy, but it was all she could think of. She could not understand it all. She only wanted to go be with Ava, wherever she was. She fell asleep, exhausted with such thoughts.

An hour or so later when she woke up, she stank and was covered in flies. They were all over her. In this part of Australia, flies were a constant source of annoyance. People furiously swatted them away from their face constantly, the boys called it the "Australian salute." A furious, writhing, maniacal swatting of the flies that were determined to land on your face and eyes and generally try to drive you insane. Those flies were on her now, all over her, all over the vomit on her face, her shirt.

As she swatted at them, she looked over at the other side of the river, but she could no longer see or hear the motorbikes. She knew the area and thought she was maybe a hundred yards down river from where she went in. She slipped down to the river's edge and tried to wash out her clothes and face as best she could of the vomit. The flies never stopped; they seemed to join in the activity, making her work even harder.

She knew what happened after the flies did their business. If you did not wash off really well, the maggots would come. She hated maggots but was also fascinated by them. All over the farm, dead things would turn into a writhing, squirming mass of maggots within days and the stink was so deliciously horrible. She did *not* want that happening to her, so she washed herself again in the river and shivered at the thought of waking up with maggots on her.

When she was done cleaning up, she finally looked around and to her great surprise found that she was not thirty yards from the old shack, Norah's old shack. It was made of wood and mud, and despite the years, still had some kind of a roof and mostly intact walls. There were plenty of holes in them, but it would be a good place to hide for a while, until she came up with a plan.

While she did not believe in ghosts, this was going to test her resolve. Here on the run, after Brett had died, another body found, and Ava just disappeared, the idea that ghosts might actually be a thing had begun to creep into her brain. Maybe there were ghosts. Maybe Ava was a ghost now, and if she went into that shack she would be attacked by the ghost of Norah and dragged back to the river and drowned.

The idea of Ava having been transported by some unseen power was just about as crazy as her becoming a ghost. It was like this with all new things you couldn't explain, the first time you see it, it seems like magic or a ghost. Maybe what Ivy had seen was just a new thing to her, but someone else seeing it might know what it was and could explain it.

But right now, for Ivy, it was a match between *Star Trek* and its transporter or ghosts moving onto the farm. Maybe even a ghost with a transporter? This idea made her laugh to herself. She kept putting the other idea out of her head, the idea that perhaps she was, in fact, going crazy.

Despite this, she walked toward the shack, such as it was, with a kind of bravery now, the kind that comes from no longer caring, or the kind that comes from having a vision and a plan that was unshakable. She would go back to the tree and find Ava or die trying, and if she died by ghost, so be it.

She needed a little more time to rest. Vomiting your guts out is exhausting, as it turned out, and she needed to breathe in a little more bravery. That bravery would come as she thought of Ava and of Brett, and the little shack seemed the perfect place to hide for a short while.

She moved cautiously toward what had been the front door, and was now just an old hinge with a piece of wood attached. She could see inside it was dark but with bright rays of light streaming through the holes in the wall. It was kind of beautiful with the little pieces of dirt lighting up in the rays of the passing light.

She moved through the door into the small space. An old bed lay on the ground, or at least what used to be an old bed, now it was more of the outline of a bed with some material that must have been a mattress remaining. Next to the bed was a tiny round table made from an old tree stump that had probably stood there for a hundred years and probably would remain for another hundred. There was nothing on the broken-down walls, nothing else on the floor now covered in dirt and leaves.

Looking around the room again, this time she noticed some words carved into the stump, covered in dust but definitely words. She walked over and brushed off the dust, seeing that the carving was old, but still readable. The first line read, *I am Norah*, the second, *The tree is the answer*. Ivy was not sure what this meant, but she knew one thing, the tree Norah was talking about must be the ring tree.

The next line Ivy read made her back up and fall over in a panic.

We are going to the tree and we will be gone.

The Picture

and the Plan

Ivy reeled back from the stump like it was a live thing, like it was talking to her. *We are going back to the tree and we will be gone.* What was this? Was it a message from all those years ago? If so, Ivy thought it must be a hundred years old. Norah had lived here back then and there were no stories of anyone else living there. None of the local kids ever went there.

And what did it mean by *gone*? Was Norah gone like Ava was gone? Why did she want to be gone, and more importantly, where was this gone place? Was there even such a place—and was she not crazy—or was this just a coincidence? *The tree is the answer,* it said. Did Norah just mean she would go to the tree and then keep going and be gone? Ivy shook her head in confusion.

Maybe it was nothing mysterious at all, just someone leaving one life for another.

Sounded like Norah needed a better life. Living on the river and doing the work she did could not have been a great life, at least not in Ivy's mind. Maybe Norah was just saying goodbye to her old shack and being gone just meant going away, not disappearing like Ava had done.

Yet Ivy thought it was something more. What she had seen at the tree she believed was real, and Ava being gone was real, for sure. What if the tree did make people go? What if Norah knew that and had decided it was time for her to go from this place altogether? The idea of where *gone* was kept coming up in Ivy's mind. She had to follow Ava wherever she had gone, there was no wavering now, but now more than ever she wondered where that was.

She needed some kind of a plan that got her back to the tree without getting stopped on the way. Though she could not hear the bikes, she was sure they were still out searching for her. Ivy, the killer. Ivy, the killer of two kids now and maybe another man. They would look for her all over, they would be at the tree, they would be down by the river, she was sure they would be everywhere.

Try as she might, she could not really think of a plan. She was on this side of the river, the tree on the other side and miles away. She had to get to the tree, climb up it, jump off and hope to disappear. Even as she thought it, that last part sounded crazy. Was this what the crazy people in the streets of the big city did all day? Stood in the road talking nonsense and thinking that people could disappear by jumping out of trees? Maybe she was going to become one of those people, maybe she was ready.

The only way to get to the tree was to wait until it was dark. On the farm, when it got dark, it got *really* dark. There were very few lights and if the moon was not shining, the only thing you could see were all the millions of stars in the sky, and there were millions. In this part of the county, her teacher said, there was no "light pollution" from big city lights so you could walk out your door and see the entire universe right above your head all the way to the horizon.

Ava and her would often stop after a long day and lie on their backs and just stare into the sky. The stars were so many, so beautiful. Ava said she could see the constellations that her teachers talked about, the southern cross, the creatures with bows and arrows and stuff. Ivy could not see these images but she loved it no less. It was all so beautiful, so shiny, so big.

Their science teacher tried to explain to them how big the universe was and she just could not get it into her head. He first told them how fast the speed of light was, how it could go around the earth seven and a half times in a second. This gave Ivy a headache. Imagine going all the way around the earth over seven times before you could even sneeze!

Then the teacher said that space is *so* big that light is kind of slow. He asked them to guess how long light takes to travel from the sun to the earth. Ivy was certain it must be just a few seconds, since light was really fast and the sun did not look that far away. The teacher said it took more than eight minutes and was nearly one hundred million miles away. One hundred million miles meant nothing to Ivy, it just sounded like a lot.

He then asked the class another question: How long do you think it would take if you had a spaceship and tried to travel to the middle of the Milky Way? They all knew the Milky Way, they saw it at night, a whole bunch of stars all squished together that lit up the sky. Ivy wanted to guess, she was getting the idea now, it had to be a lot longer than eight minutes, so she guessed two hours. She thought that was a crazy amount of time to go so fast, but she was caught up in excitement of it all. Other kids made their guesses, one saying it would take a year, and the entire class started laughing. The teacher took a big breath and said 25,000 years.

The class went silent. Before the time of pyramids (they had just done this in class), before Jesus, before Mohammad, before Moses, before all the cities in the world had been made. Thousands of years before the white people came to this country, or most countries. Only the original people of this place had lived here 25,000 years ago. There was no Melbourne or Sydney or Paris or London or Cairo or anything that looked like this time. If they all left now, in that spaceship going at light speed, 25,000 years would pass before they got to the center of the Milky Way.

Then he dropped the next bomb: "And that is just our part of the universe!" There were millions of Milky Ways in the universe and they were millions, and billions, of years away. With that, the bell rang and the kids went to break and somehow never felt quite the same afterwards. Sometimes, a good class and a great teacher could do that to you. Make you leave a class a different person than when you entered.

Ivy snapped back from this memory from not so long ago, before Brett had gone, before all the kids hated her and Ava. This was all she could come up with: go at night, sneak to the tree, don't get caught. Without the moon it was so dark that at first, you could see nothing, not even a few feet in front of you. But Ivy knew the moon was at least a little bit out, so if she gave her eyes long enough, she would be able to see a little.

She knew this place so well she knew she could make it to the tree even though she almost never went there. This was her place, the one she and Ava knew like no one else. She could make it. Then she remembered where she was. The wrong side of the river!

Her shoulders slumped. She would have to cross the river again, and soon, because she could never do it in the dark. Just the thought of it was almost enough to make her give up. That river had nearly killed her, now she would have to cross it again. At least she knew she could do it, but she had to find a narrower place to get across.

The rope tree! In the time before Brett had gone, some of the older kids had strung a rope across a branch of a tall tree and would swing over the river and the bravest, or stupidest, would let go and splash into the river. After Brett disappeared, no one felt like doing it, but Ivy thought that if she swung hard enough, she could get most of the way across.

Then she remembered the rope was on the other side of the river. That was not going to work. But near that rope tree, she recalled, there was another big old tree that had fallen into the river and was nearly all the way across. She was sure it was at the narrowest part of the river near here, and she started to get up. It was now or never.

As she stood, she reached out her hand to get her balance as the leaves on the floor were slippery. She felt something on the floor, something she had not seen until then, something hidden by the leaves. When she looked closer, she saw it was a picture, one of those old-timey pictures in black and white. She always found those pictures creepy with the strange-looking people never smiling and in those crazy old clothes. She figured it must be very old, from the time of Norah. All covered in dirt and sitting on the ground for all these years.

She brushed it off, and to her amazement, there was still an image there. As always, the image showed people standing up and looking quite awkward. She brushed at it some more and brought it closer to see what they looked like. For a second, she paused, then caught her breath and dropped the picture in terror, backing quickly into a corner to get as far from it as possible. She had never been so afraid, not even close.

After a time of cowering in the corner, she decided what she had seen must not be real. Her imagination must have played a trick on her. She felt more and more like she was becoming one of the crazy people. She made her way back to the picture, and picked it up at arm's length, like there was some kind of dangerous spider sitting on it she meant to flick out the door. She moved it closer to her face with trembling fingers.

Just four people, that was all. A tall beautiful woman and a little girl, maybe two or three years old. Nothing strange there. Then she looked at the other figures and dropped the picture again. She shivered and took a deep breath. How could it be? She was equal parts scared, amazed, and terribly sad.

Next to the child was a girl about her age and an old man. The girl she knew immediately. The way she stood, the flow of her hair, the expression on her face. It was Ava. There was no denying it. The old man looked familiar, too, and she was sure she knew him, but she could not quite place him. As if all of this was not weird enough, there was another person in the picture. It was her.

She rubbed her eyes, she rubbed the picture, she looked at it from all sides and the top, but no matter how she tried, she could not erase the image of her friend from this ancient picture, or the girl that looked like her. How could this be? This picture had to be from Norah's time, from before Ava and her parents had lived, before their even grandparents had lived. Yet here they were in front of her!

The clothes were way too long and flowy with way too many frills, like the clothing from the old westerns that showed on TV late at night. Brett had died six months ago, Ava had disappeared yesterday, she was sitting right here, so how could there be a picture of her and Ava together from so long ago?

Ivy was smart, so her brain went into overtime to try and explain it, and there was only one explanation that made sense. These must be long-lost relatives of theirs. Kids that in their time looked just like them, but were not them. Kids that went on to grow up and have their own kids, then these kids grew up and had kids, and on and on, until Ava and her came along and looked just like their ancient relatives. With this somewhat logical explanation, she started to feel better. She felt relieved, too, and a bit silly for being so afraid. Until she looked again, closer this time.

What she saw kicked Ivy's brain into overdrive. There was no way to explain this. It was Ava's hand—she took a deep breath—Ava's left hand hung by her side, and her fingers made the shape of a reverse "C." Ivy knew this sign very well. Over the years, Ivy and Ava had made up their own sign language after they saw a show on TV about how deaf kids communicated using hand signs. They tried to learn the proper signs but gave up, it was too hard and there was no one to help them. Instead, they made up their own signs that only they could understand. They used it all the time, a silent language just between them. It was one of their many secrets.

That reverse, low-down "C" was only to be seen by them, and it meant "come to me." It could be used just for fun or when one of them was in trouble, but the meaning was clear. And with that revelation, Ivy was again terrified. Here, in an old-timey picture from who knows when, with three strangers she also did not know, was Ava flashing a sign only they knew, asking Ivy to come. Was Ava scared? Was she okay? Where was she, *when* was she?

Ivy looked past the people at the background and saw a big old building that looked like an old church. Around the church were people milling about and a very old lady that stood out. Ivy could not say why she stood out, exactly, except that this old lady was looking right at the camera, right at Ivy.

None of this could be real, none of this could be right. Ivy thought she must be losing her mind. Or, she was just missing a piece of the puzzle that made it all fit together and make sense, and she had not thought of it yet.

She did not know what to do with the picture. It seemed like it was just for her, but was it right to take it? What if someone else came to this place—did this picture belong to the shack? Maybe if she took it, she could find someone who could tell her if it was real, whatever real meant. Maybe like the shows on TV they could tell her how old it was.

She looked at it again and she knew she had to leave it. It was so old it was already starting to fall apart around the edges. It would never make the trip she was about to take, especially across the river.

She put it on the stump next to the message and hoped one day soon to come back with Ava and look at it together, when it would all be explained and make sense.

The light was starting to fade. Time to make her way to the river and find a way across that looked like the easiest swim. She left the shack, but as she did so, she took one last look, wishing she had found more answers here. Yes, the stump carvings had confirmed she must go back to the tree. And the picture, too, must surely hold some secret message for her that she just couldn't make out yet. What was this place? What was that message?

She felt so terribly alone without Ava by her side. She wished she could go home to her mother, the old mother she remembered from the past. The one that cuddled her and sang with her and made her feel safe. She had not seen that mother in a long time, not since she first started school, she thought. Yet she so desperately wished that mother still lived in the house on the hill. But she did not, she had gone, and all Ivy had left was a vague memory, and of course, Ava.

Now Ava was gone but she would find her again, she was sure of it. It was not until that moment that she wondered why Ava had gone without her. Why did she seem to have just left her behind? She knew in her heart Ava would not do this normally, that she needed Ivy as much as she needed her. And hadn't Ava's last words to her in the tree, before she jumped, before she disappeared, been, "You should come"? What if Ava needed her now?

This thought made her panic, wondering if Ava was somehow abducted. Had the ghost with the transporter unit tricked Ava into going and leaving Ivy behind? Maybe she was not just somewhere else, maybe she was in trouble, big trouble! Imagining Ava needing her help gave her all the extra bravery she needed. She quickly closed the door behind her and headed for the river.

At the river bank, she looked over to the other side again to check that no one was close. When she did not see anyone, she headed to the rope swing. It was not too far away but when she got there, she froze. Across the river, two men were looking around. She saw a little boat and figured they must have made their way up the river in it, though she had not heard its tiny engine. There was no doubt they were looking for her, and before she could even duck for cover, they saw her and started calling her name to stop.

She ran. They kept calling after her and she kept running, running along the bank back toward the shack. She heard the boat now, and this time it must have been going at full speed because there was no missing the noise of the engine. It was clear as day. She ran as fast as she could but they were getting closer.

Ahead of her was a large tree with the trunk broken off halfway and tilted at an angle. The root at the bottom was pulling up. She recognized this sight. This tree was dead and doing the slow fall that often took years as the roots pulled up and finally gave away, toppling the rest of the tree over.

She could see a hole at the base of the tree where the old roots had been, and at full speed, she jumped like a long jumper in the Olympics and landed in it. She stuck the landing with a thump and was now under the level of the ground around her, not by much, but enough so she could peek over without being seen.

The noise of the boat was quieting now, they were slowing down and they were close. She made herself as small as possible, lying as flat to the bottom of the tree as she could. Then she looked up and saw it.

This was a hollow tree, the most mysterious and rare of trees around the river. It had died long ago but still stood, if only just. The middle of the tree had rotted and been eaten by all kinds of critters and now was hollow in the middle. Her mother had told her about such trees and warned her to stay away.

They seemed so exciting to get up inside, but they were full of spiders and snakes and might fall over, so you better stay out of them, she had been told. Ava and Ivy had only ever found two like it but they never went in. They weren't so afraid of spiders, they were a constant part of life on the farm, but being in the dark in a hollow tree with spiders and critters did not seem like too much fun, so they never ventured in. Not until today.

Behind and slightly above her she heard the men coming her way, talking, but she could not make out the words. She was going to get caught for sure unless she made her way into the hollow tree trunk. This was a time to do, not a time to think.

She slipped herself first down to the opening of the hollow, then up into the trunk. It was a little tight but not too tight. The good news was she was sure that a full-grown man could not follow her, so she made her way up a little more so they could not see her.

As she went further up, at first it got a lot darker and scarier, but a little higher she saw the light coming from the top of the tree and she got less scared. It seemed to her to be about five or ten feet to the top, about the size she was, maybe by twice. Then she heard the men yelling.

They were now at the base of the tree and must have seen her tracks, for she heard them at the bottom calling out to her to come out. "We know you are in there, come out, now!" This made her even more sure that coming out was a bad idea. Their voices were not calm, or caring, their voices were excited, like they had caught a creature that they planned to do no good with.

She had heard that tone from her brother and the adults that would come to the farm on their shooting sprees to kill the Galahs and other birds they decided would make good target practice. It was the tone of men on the hunt, only now she was the hunted and she was the prize. She felt a tug on her shoe.

One of the men had gotten into the hole and was reaching up into the hollow, grabbing at her foot. She kicked him off and went scrambling up further into the tree. Far enough up to get away from his hand, but not too far as to pop out the top. The voices did not stop. They were becoming louder, more excited, now that they had their prey. She was so close, they just had to scare her out.

For what seemed like forever, nothing happened. The yelling stopped and she could hear them talking, but she could not make it out. Then she smelled something she knew very well. Burning old eucalyptus leaves, at first a little waft up the tree trunk, then more and more smoke. They were literally smoking her out, like a rat!

They must have made a little fire at the base of the tree and were burning leaves. They yelled up at her that they could either stop the fire and let her come out, or they could just make it bigger and "smoke your ass out of there."

She was so scared, so alone. She did not want to face them, they sounded mean, angry, and she had to get away. The smoke stopped for a short time, then it started again, this time much worse. So much smoke, it was getting hard to breath. But the short break had given her an idea, her only idea.

Since this tree was next to the river, if she scrambled to the top she could jump out and into the water. And if she was lucky, maybe she could make it to the other side before they realized she was gone. Did they know it was hollow all the way through? If not, they would soon, the smoke must be coming out the top by now. There was no other way, no other choice. She was sure to get caught but she had to try! If she stayed here, she was sure she would die.

She made her way up the trunk, coughing now and gagging as the smoke got worse and worse. The light above her grew brighter until she was just under the opening at the top of the tree. She just had to push herself out and jump out into the water, then swim as fast as she could to the other side and hope they were too slow to catch her before she made it.

Without another thought, she made her move. She scaled higher, got to the edge, found a great foothold, then burst into the light and jumped with all her might toward the river.

BACK AT THE
RING TREE

I vy did not land in the water as she had hoped, but with a thud and a crackle on branches and leaves. She was confused. Had she miscalculated the short distance between the tree and the river? She hadn't made it to the river's edge, she must have fallen straight down to the ground beneath the hollow tree.

She had lost her breath and was winded, unable to take another. Just like that time the girl in year ten had hit her hard in the stomach and she could not breathe at all for a minute. She rolled over, trying to catch a breath, and then she saw it, plain as day, right above her. Suddenly, she stopped worrying about taking a breath.

Right above her, not ten feet away, was the lower branch of the ring tree. She had landed on the bed of leaves and branches that Ava and her had made the day before. She had missed the river, but not because she did not jump far enough, she had jumped at least two miles! With that realization, she coughed and vomited and took a breath and thought, for sure, this time, she was now officially one of the crazy ones.

What was happening here? Why had she been transported to this very tree? *How* had she? This must be what happened to Ava. First in one place then, *boom,* transported to another. If this was true, she now knew of two places that could do this. The ring tree and the hollow tree. How many more were there? What were they, and what purpose did they have? Again, her brain started to hurt from the sheer confusion of it all.

For what felt like the longest time, she lay there as the coughing stopped and the breathing came back. She looked around, and to her fright, saw a motorbike a few hundred meters away in a little brush area. She knew that area and what was probably happening. It was the local "bathroom" where Ava had gone just yesterday, a perfect place for a little alone time in a paddock without much cover. Someone was stationed at the tree to catch her if she returned, but nature had called and they were, for now, distracted.

She looked around for the prize, and there it was laying on the ground. The ladder made of leaves and branches. She jumped up and raced toward it, then started to raise it toward the lower branch. It was not too heavy but really awkward. She steadied herself behind it and started to walk her hands up it as it raised itself higher into the air and closer to the lower branch.

Hearing the motor bike start up, she panicked. They would be here in just a few moments! She pushed the ladder to the tree, it caught, and she started up it as fast as she could without breaking any of the rungs, though a few started to give away as she moved quickly, pulling apart at the bottom just as she was almost to the top.

When the ladder started to fall, with one quick move she jumped to the hollow knot and caught it with both hands. She hung now in midair, no ladder, it was on the ground in pieces.

The bike was really close now. Ivy started to pull herself up. Every year, the school did a fitness test, and being able to do two chin-ups in her age group was the national standard. Ivy thought this was funny, just two. Most of the girls in her class could not even do one yet, their bodies had not yet packed on the muscles required for such a feat. But Ivy could do two, no problem. In fact, she held the school record for her age and could do nearly ten. She had been climbing the trees here since she could walk and doing chin-ups was a daily part of the practice.

But a chin-up alone was not going to be enough. She had to do a "power move," they called it on one of the TV shows with all those athletes running, jumping, and climbing against each other. Shows that one day she thought she could win. The power move was to do a chin-up so fast and hard that you could hoist your body or leg onto the next level. So with all her might, she pulled up and swung her leg to the closest lowest part of the lower branch. She caught it then started to wriggle her leg further across the branch. She heard a new sound then, and the rocks came.

The kookaburras had gone from zero to full chorus, it was quiet one minute and deafening the next. They had obviously just noticed the excitement and wanted to join in. At the same time, she felt a sharp stab in her back, then again, then one on her head. She realized these were rocks, rocks being pelted by someone below. Thrown really hard.

"I caught you, Ivy the gay! Ivy the murderer! I got you!" yelled the menacing voice she knew so well.

This was Mac, "Big Mac," most called him. He had gotten really big in the eighth grade and earned the nickname, but then he stopped growing, and while he was still big, he was not the monster-sized guy his brother was. Maybe this is why Big Mac was so mean. He had graduated from school, well, not graduated but left the year before, but the memories and stories of his meanness were legend at the Central School.

Big Mac delighted in making other kids, the younger kids in particular, cower in fear and dread. He loved to make them cry, he got energy from being the bad guy and he played the role so well. Ivy had avoided him as best she could, but she watched him hit, punch, pull, name call and generally terrorize the little kids for years before he left the school. The day he did not turn up to school was one of great relief on the school grounds.

Mac was not the only bully in the school, but he was certainly one of the best at the craft. He was about six feet tall with long blond hair and a scar on his right cheek. A big one. The stories about this scar were also legendary, but it turned out this was a present from his older brother. Mac had tried to tell people he got it from a street fight with a bunch of out-of-town guys that he had taken out. But his brother made the real story clear. "You were being a little bitch so I shut you up!"

All the kids had laughed, but not Ivy and Ava. They knew when you embarrassed a bully, the weak and smaller would pay. They slunk to the back of the crowd, to hide from Mac's gaze and his oh-so-certain revenge. Not that it really mattered, he took out that anger on anyone he felt he could torture without getting caught. He was that kid, now nearly a full-grown man and pelting rocks at Ivy just as hard as he could.

Ivy had made it to the lower branch now. The rocks kept coming and she felt a warm trickle down her neck, which a wipe of her hand confirmed was blood. One of the rocks had hit her pretty squarely in the head and she swore she could feel the skin pull apart under the weight and speed of it hitting her scalp.

Now what to do? She had come all this way, made it to the tree, was enduring rocks and insults, but was not sure now what to do next. What was she thinking? Ava had disappeared, but it still made no sense. How would she disappear? Did Ava say some magic words or do some incantation or something? She looked down and beside her on the branch was the strangest sight.

A kookaburra stood next to her, nonplussed, staring at her. She had never seen one so up-close, so unfazed by a human within range. It looked at her, tilted its head, then looked out over the fields and the river then back to her. Then it jumped, flapped its wings for a moment, and then came back down on the branch. Underneath it zoomed a rock, which somehow it had seen coming from behind and done a little jump and dance move to dodge the incoming missile.

It looked at Ivy again, then out across the land. It repeated this action as Ivy caught a rock to the thigh and almost fell backward. She then realized, or at least thought she did, that this animal, this native of this strange and wonderful land, was talking to her. In sign language, it was telling her to jump toward the field in front of them. Again, it did its look at her, then over the land and back, and Ivy swore she could read the expression on its face. It was like this old, calm and wise bird face, looking at her, then out to the field and back, was telling her to *jump*.

The rocks were coming faster now and Ivy realized that Big Mac must no longer be alone. Suddenly, she heard a loud *crack*. It made Ivy jump, but not the kookaburra. She knew it was a gun, and when she looked down, sure enough, Big Mac was joined by a man with a rifle. It was not pointed at her, it was pointed up, as though making a point that next it could be headed her way.

The next moment, the rifle was indeed pointed at her as the man yelled, "Time to get down, kid, or the next round is in your butt! And trust me, you do not want that!"

Ivy was panicking now. Rocks were one thing, a bullet was a whole other problem. She had watched animals get shot, the damage and the death those bullets brought were gruesome, and she did not want one of those hitting her even in the butt!

She looked again at the kookaburra, also a bit more frantic now, looking at her and back out over the horizon but in a faster cadence. The arrival of the gun made the next step easy.

Ivy glanced over at the bird one more time and mouthed the words "thank you" to it, though she was not sure why and was sure it could not lip read. She then looked out into the distance, pictured her dear Ava, and like her, spread her arms wide and leapt forward into the sky ahead.

She braced herself for impact, but it never came. What came was far stranger than anything she had experienced before. The horizon disappeared, the river was no more, and surrounding her were the night, the stars, and the falling ever faster.

The Other Place

The sensation of falling was all around her, faster and faster, the stars at first sitting as they always did in the sky, now racing faster and faster past her. Why were the stars out so early? Ivy wondered, but that was not the strangest of it. They started moving so fast it was like they were in a tunnel, and she was speeding past the stars.

Time seemed to stop, or go fast, or neither, or perhaps both. It was like a dream but not like a dream. A dream where you are fully awake and know it is a dream, but could not for the life of you wake up.

She tried to wake herself but then she landed on solid ground. Except it was not solid ground, it was a tree limb. At first, she thought she must have landed back on the ring tree, but as she looked around, she realized she was not on the farm anymore. Or at least, no part of the farm she had ever seen, and that was impossible, as she had been to every part of the farm.

This tree she had landed in was no ring tree. It was much bigger, with branches all above her forming something like a giant tent. The leaves above blocked most of the sun but it was still warm and comfortable. She could see the giant roots of the tree below her, but most amazingly, out in the distance was no river but rather an ocean, a big, beautiful ocean. So blue, but glistening with shiny white reflections of the sun. She had seen the ocean just once near Melbourne, and in books, but she was sure she had never seen anything so wonderful as this. She could also see a wharf jetting into the water and people, far off, walking on that wharf.

The wonder of the moment was only a reprieve for what came next—total and complete confusion. Where was she, how did she get here, where was the farm, the river, the bird? What was this place, where was this place, when was this place? As all this started swirling in her brain, she knew the next step must be getting down from the tree.

The branch where she had landed was up high and jumping off was not an option, but toward the trunk of the tree she saw a way down. It would require some climbing, but the roots of the tree made their way up the trunk and formed a kind of a trunk-root ladder with lots of foot and hand holds that would get the job done. That is, if you were an expert tree climber, and this she was.

She made her way to the bottom of the tree and looked up from where she had come from. She was not sure why, but was certain she would need to know exactly what branch to get back to one day. If there was a way back to the farm that branch was the key, she knew it in her bones.

So, she memorized that branch and the way back up, the foot and hand holds, closing her eyes and practicing it again and again until it was a map in her head that could not be erased.

Having done the work of map making she looked around and saw nothing familiar. The tree stood out as the biggest thing in the area, the ocean a few hundred meters away. A street ran between the tree and the ocean, and she saw an old-timey car go by, the kind she had seen only in movies and pictures. The lady driving it had on a big frilly hat and gloves and looked like she was going to a dress-up party. The car smoked as it went by and backfired a few times along the way.

"What are you wearing?" A voice from behind her made her start. "You not from around here, are you?"

The voice came from the side of the tree, in a nook, where an old woman sat knitting an item Ivy could not make out. She looked impossibly old, older than humans should be, with deep lines in her face and most of her teeth missing. Yet she spoke clearly, if not for a little slur over some of the words, no doubt from all the excess of gums where her teeth should be.

"Nope, you not from around here but I saw those clothes before, I have. I saw them right here, I have. Seen them before, I have..." She went on as if Ivy were not actually there, or as if she were a statue showing off her apparently unique clothing line.

The women herself had on a long flowing skirt and a shirt and jacket, which seemed to Ivy way too much clothing to be wearing on such a warm day. And they were, of course, she thought to herself, old timey just like the car.

"Yep, I saw them before, right here, I saw them. Seen the people just like you as well." On she went, paying no mind to whether Ivy was listening or not. "I sit here all day, you see, I work here all day and I see all the things around here. I sit right here in this tree and I grow old with this tree, I do. We grow old together, we do."

As she went on, Ivy was sure she was not even talking to her now.

"I've been here since this tree was planted, you see, right from the beginning, right from when it came off the boat. Right on that day that sailor man gave the seed to me. Then Ava came."

Ivy jumped. What did she say? Whose name did she use?

"He gave it right to me, I planted it, and later Ava came."

"Wait, what was her name, the girl, what was her name?" Ivy almost cried. The old woman looked at her with a start, like it was the first time she saw her.

"Ava, Ava's her name. She is a strange one, our Ava, but she is a good one. Not too many like our Ava," the old lady professed.

"How do you know her? Where is she? Where is Ava now?" Ivy was stumbling over her words, at this tree, in this place. She was sure this old lady's Ava was her Ava and she must find her, or she was sure she would go mad, maybe like this old lady.

"I planted it right where the old Indian lady told me to plant it. She knows just where to plant it, right next to some painted rock she said her ancestors made. Right next to them, we planted it together. She said it was a special place that her ancestors had known about before the white people came."

She kept on making no sense to Ivy but she was not interested in that story right now, only in finding Ava. "Where is Ava?" Ivy pleaded. "Where is she? I must see her!"

"Oh, she is not here, she is up on the hill, in the shed, I expect, in the horse shed on the hill. She spends a lot of time in the shed with her friends, you know, the ones that don't grow old." She paused as if in thought then continued, "Yes, I am sure she is in the shed. She looks after the horses, you know, and they let her sleep right there in the shed with them. She gets to stay in that shed if she looks after the horses, she does."

I must find that shed, Ivy thought, *I must find it right now.* She was almost in a panic. "Where is this shed? I must go find her! Can you tell me where it is?" Ivy pleaded.

"Up on the hill, about a mile over there." The old lady pointed behind her absently. "Don't worry though, love, Ava comes here every day. She comes right here to talk to me and the tree, every day. She will be here soon, I expect, about that time of day right now. I expect she will be along soon." The old lady again seemed to be talking to herself.

"What does she look like?" Ivy asked the old lady.

"Well, she looks just like you, of course!" she muttered in a tone that seemed a little irritated. "She said you would come, she said you would," she continued. "'Cept she did say that many years ago when we were both young girls. Ava still looks like you, she does, just like you. She said you would come and I believed her, I did, all these years, Ava didn't lie. She is strange, but she is no liar."

Ivy tried to interrupt with another question but the old lady was again ranting to herself.

"She don't lie, she don't get old, and she lives on the hill, these are all facts, they are. Came here a long time ago when we were girls, she did, met her right here, I did. Been friends ever since. Long time ago, that was, but I remember it like it was not so long ago."

The lady chuckled to herself, knitting and staring into the distance. "She wasn't the first, though, there were a few others. A boy, a lady and her kid. They came first, you know, then Ava."

She was on a roll now, Ivy couldn't have stopped her if she tried.

"They all live in that shed, you know, they all live there and they work there. They say they come from another place, but they like this place..." she trailed off, momentarily thoughtful. "I 'spect they will go back, though, no good to stay here so long. Least that is what the old Indian lady said, 'No good to stay too long,' she told me, that was before she left to go north."

None of this was making sense to Ivy, but she was now too afraid to interrupt, in case the woman said something that made more sense of this place.

Then the old lady sat up in a flash. "Here she comes right now, just like I said!"

Ivy followed her gaze, and coming around the corner, out near the ocean, appeared a girl right around her age, wearing a weird dress that did not hide her true identity. Ava! Ivy started running.

As Ivy got closer the truth became clearer and her heart grew lighter. It was Ava, just like she had been just yesterday. Ava in an old-timey dress, but it was Ava for sure. Ivy started yelling to her and Ava started to sprint, right toward Ivy, both running as fast as they could. They crashed into each other and fell to the ground.

"Ivy, is that you? Is that really you?" Ava asked in a tearful voice, as though afraid to believe her own eyes. "Can it really be you? Is this real? It's been so long, so very long, Ivy, please tell me it is you!"

"Ava, it's me! I'm right here! Why are you confused? It's me, right here, I followed you. I followed you after you disappeared yesterday. Took me a whole day to find you but I did!" Ivy pronounced.

Ava fell back, like she had seen a ghost. "How long have I been gone, Ivy?" she asked in a quiet voice now.

"Just a day, Ava, just a day or so. I followed you here. I thought I had gone crazy, maybe I am, but you sure look real!"

Ava grew very quiet now. "Oh my, oh my," she started to mutter.

"What's wrong? It was just a day! I got here as fast as I could, just like you, though the ring tree, right through it, that's how I came to this place," Ivy said.

"Oh my, so long, so long, so very long..." Ava continued as though in a trance.

Ivy frowned, confused. "Not that long, just a day or so. I had to swim across the river, nearly died crossing that river, and I went to Norah's place. I went to the shack!" she said excitedly.

Ava snapped out of her trance at the sound of Norah's name. "She's here, Ivy, Norah is here in this place! I live with her and Sharron. We have lived here a very long time."

Ivy shook her head in disbelief.

"Ivy, we have been here for many years, a lot of years, a whole lifetime of years!" Ava persisted, wide-eyed. "And there's more, something more..." And she trailed off.

Ivy could not grasp what Ava was telling her. What did she mean, a whole lifetime of years? She didn't understand. Didn't Ava just fall from the ring tree yesterday?

"Ava, what happened when you first got here?" Ivy asked with wide eyes.

Ava in Wonderland

The sensation of speed and light came to an abrupt end as Ava landed with a gentle thump on the ground next to a tree. Dazed, she ran her hand over her head and arms to make sure she was awake. She looked around in shock, seeing she was not on the farm but by a beach, with the smell of sea in the air and a small town just inland.

The tree next to her was not the ring tree she had just climbed up, but she recognized it as some kind of a fig. She had seen these kinds of trees in books about Australia, so she thought she must still be close to home. As she was catching her breath, she heard a girl's voice, shocked and somewhat scared, from just behind the tree.

"Where did you come from?" the girl asked.

Ava stood up and to her great surprise saw a girl about her age lying in the grass, apparently trying to hide from her.

"You just appeared! How did you do that?" the young girl pleaded with her. "I ain't never see anything like that. Are you some kind of a ghost?"

"No, I…I don't know how I got here," Ava said. The girl continued to stare at her, a little less scared now, Ava thought.

"And what are those crazy clothes you got on, you a Indian or something? I never seen clothes like that even on the Indian people here."

She kept on, not waiting for an answer before asking another question. Ava realized she was one of those people that liked to talk when they were anxious, peppering you with questions you never had time to answer, perhaps in the hope that these questions would stop you from saying or doing something to frighten them.

"And why do you sound so funny? You don't talk like people around here," she went on.

Before the girl could ask yet more questions, Ava cut her off with her own. "Where is this place? I don't recognize it. What beach is that?" she asked as she pointed out to the ocean.

"Well, why would you ask that? You came here, you just appeared, so you must be some kind of a ghost and you would think a ghost would know such things."

Again, Ava jumped in, realizing that one had to be quick with this one or get pelted with more and more questions. "I am no ghost," she declared, "just a girl like you. But somehow, I just arrived at this place from my farm. My name is Ava, what's yours?"

"My name is Adeline," the girl replied, pleased to see that this ghost, if she was that, was at least a friendly one.

"What is the name of this place, Adeline? Where is it?" Ava continued, taking over the questioning.

"Well, it has a few names. The local Indians call this place Syukhtun, but the Mexicans and the English folk call it Santa Barbara," Adeline answered.

"Santa Barbara, where is that? I've never heard of it," Ava announced in a disbelieving tone.

"That's what they call it. I've been here for a few years now, my father works on one of those boats. Trading boat, it is, trading all kinds of things, but I don't get to see him much."

She pointed to a boat anchored out in the water off the beach. "We came with him a few years back and decided to stay, to help build up the place, my momma said. Stay here with the Indians and Mexicans and make a new life right here near the beach. It's a lovely place, always sunny, except when it rains and the fog comes in, but mostly always sunny…"

Adeline was getting on a roll again, Ava saw, so she jumped back in. "But where is this place? Where is this Santa Barbara? What part of Australia is this?" she asked, a little frustrated.

"What?" Adeline asked and started to giggle. "This is not Australia. Though I know about that place, my momma told me about it. She's a teacher here in the school house and she knows lots of things," the girl proudly announced.

"Not Australia? How can that be, that tree right there, that tree is from Australia!" Ava pointed to the tree next to them that she has seen in Australian picture books.

"Oh, that is a tree from Australia, you are right! A sailor gave my momma a seed and we planted it right here and it has grown up real well, just like me. My momma said it is a Morton Bay Fig, from some place in Australia called Morton Bay, I guess. But it sure loves this place and is growing up real fast."

Adeline looked lovingly at the tree. "I come here most every day to sit and read my books and watch the ocean and the people. And then, *boom*, you just appeared and I got so scared I hid right in this grass! I did not even have time to run away!"

Ava shook her head no, like she wanted the girl to stop talking and go back to the part about not this not being Australia. "If we're not in Australia, then where are we?" she asked, exasperated.

"Well, this is America! Though it used to be Mexico and Spain, my momma said, and before that it was Indian land. Now it is America, 'the far west' my momma calls it. This place right here people call California," the girl stated in a way that suggested most people might not know such things.

Ava sat down with a start. "California! How can that be? California is so far from Australia!" She knew California, that was where Disneyland was, a place she and Ivy had decided would be one of their first trips together when they were older. California, Disneyland, they were thousands of miles away, hours and hours in a jet plane. California!

"What year is this?" Ava blurted out before Adeline had a chance to say more.

"What kind of a ghost are you?" the girl started in again, but Ava shut her down somewhat crossly

"I told you, I am not a ghost! Just a girl like you! What year is this?" Ava demanded.

"Well, it's 1877, of course!"

With that, Ava went silent. For some reason, she did not even question whether it was true. The whole thing just seemed true: the ring tree, the bird, the travel, the girl, the beach, and now this. She had fallen into wonderland and had no idea why, but had no delusions that it was not all, in fact, true.

REUNION

Ivy listened to Ava's story without saying a word, though it didn't make any sense to her. "But Ava, you disappeared just yesterday! It was not that long ago, and you look the same, so it can't be much time that's passed."

Even as Ivy said it, she did notice something different about Ava. Oh, she was still Ava, still pretty and young just like Ivy, but something was different. It was in her eyes, they had changed and looked more like an adult's eyes now. Like they had seen lots of things that a young girl had not seen.

"I've been here a long time, Ivy, many years. I've been waiting for you for so many years! I knew you would come, but it's been so long, so very long." And with this, Ava hugged Ivy with all her might and started sobbing a deep, deep sob, her whole body moving up and down.

Ivy felt crushed by the force of it but she did not stop her. Ava seemed so very sad, like she had never seen her before, but also happy somehow. Ivy did not understand that. How could a person be so sad and happy at the same time? But Ava was both right now, she could feel it.

"Ivy, it's been so long and I knew you would come, but I didn't know when. I waited here, and kept coming back to this tree for you all these years. I never left, I never forgot the farm, I never forgot *you*! Not once, not one day. I can't believe you're here, Ivy, I just can't believe it after all this time! You came, you came back to me!"

Ava was crying even more now. Ivy did not understand why she was so happy-sad, why she was crying so much, when it had just been a day. She got here as fast as she could!

After a long time, Ava let Ivy go but still held her hand. They had sat down together on the grass and Ava lay back, holding onto Ivy's hand like it was a life raft, like if she let go, Ivy would run off.

"Ava," Ivy asked in a small, scared voice, "where are we?"

Ava did not answer at first, she just held Ivy's hand and looked up into the sky. After a time, she said, "Ivy, you're not going to believe this at first, and I think you have to see it. Telling you doesn't work. I could not believe it for a very long time. We're a long way from home, an ocean away, but that's not even the strangest part. We're also a long time from home. This is not our time, this is olden times, years before we were even born, Ivy."

Ivy lay back on the grass too, looking up at the same sky as Ava. She was trying to believe her best friend, but it all seemed so impossible.

"We're an ocean and years away from the farm. And not just us, Ivy, there are others from other places and other times. It seems like this is where some people come from all around. People come here for a while to rest. Seems like the tree is how they get here, then they stay for a time in the town," Ava continued.

Ivy stayed quiet, just listening.

"Ivy, I've been here for many years, seeing people come and go, but I stayed. I waited for you. I wasn't sure if I should go back. Would it be the right time? I didn't even know how! Maybe someone knows, so I waited for you all these years. I missed you so much, Ivy, I missed you my whole life!" And with that Ava started to cry again, this time quietly, and mostly just the sad kind of crying not the happy-sad kind from moments before.

Ivy rolled over and put her arm over Ava. She did not understand everything she was talking about, but she knew her friend was very sad. She whispered in her ear, "I am here now, Ava, and I am not going anywhere. We're together again, and we will be forever."

They lay there for the longest time, Ivy next to her friend, Ava exhausted from all the emotions. She held Ivy's hand and fell asleep for a time, like being awake was too much to bear. She slept while Ivy held her hand and thought about all of the things Ava had said.

When Ava woke, she rubbed her eyes and sat up. "Ivy," she announced "I have to show you where we are. It's a beautiful place! I have some good friends here and there's so much to tell you. I have horses now! Well, they're not mine but I get to look after them. Oh, Ivy, I can't believe you're here, I have so much to show you!"

Ava stood up and Ivy followed her as she headed back to the Morton Bay Fig tree where Ivy had arrived, just a short walk from where they had run to meet each other.

"Adeline!" Ava called out as they approached the tree. "Adeline, this is my friend Ivy I have been telling you about all these years. This is my cousin Ivy from the farm!"

The old lady looked up from her knitting. "I 'spected it was Ivy. She looks just like you. With those same silly clothes you used to wear," she chuckled softly. "Welcome, Ivy. Ava said you would come and I believed her. Well, for the first few years anyway, then I suspected Ava was a little crazy and I still do!"

Apparently, Adeline found this very amusing and started to cackle. "I suspect you is crazy, all right, but the fact that she is still a little girl now and I am a old lady must mean I'm the crazy one, I 'spect." Adeline continued to make herself laugh at the thought of it.

"Adeline is the first person I met here, Ivy, the very first all those years ago. I met her right here under the tree, though the tree was a lot smaller then, right, Adeline?"

"Indeed, it was, just a small thing back then. Been more than seventy years, I guess. This tree grows slow but it grows real big, this tree, real big. It ain't no normal tree, this one, this is a special tree. Might be the only tree like it in the world, this tree. People come from all over to see this tree, they just show up, just like you girls did. Just show up, they do, from all over the world, they do. Then they go back, they all go back. Well, almost all. Ava never went back, Norah never went back, or her daughter, or that other friend of yours, Ava. You all stayed and I got old!" Adeline let out another cackle.

"Adeline, we're going up to the shed, you need anything?" Ava asked.

"I got all I need, Ava. Got to finish off these socks, I do, for Miss Brinkenhoff. She is a mean one, got to get them done or hear her complaining. Can't stand to hear people complain, got to get this one done, Ava," Adeline noted and went right back to knitting, not looking up as she said, "Good to meet you, Miss Ivy. I will be seeing you soon, I'm sure. This tree sure is a strange one."

Ava led Ivy toward a hill in the distance, passing through a small town between them and the hill. A very strange town, from olden times, full of people from olden times with suits and flowing gowns and old-time stinky cars. Yet it was a beautiful city, full of life and people and rich with the smell of the ocean.

Down by the ocean was a big hotel and right across the front it said "The California Hotel." In and out its doors came all the old-timey people, talking and wearing their way-too-long dresses, though they looked wonderful to

Ivy. She felt again like she was in a dream, this time a dream about a far-off land from long ago. She had seen pictures and even movies on TV from this time. She thought maybe this was a movie set. She had heard that in America they had big movie sets and they could make it look like any place you wanted.

As she walked with Ava up a street called "State" she soon realized this could not be a movie set. It was too big, too many doing normal things. Walking and talking, eating breakfast, reading newspapers. As she walked past one man, she could see the date on the paper plain as the day, it said *June 28, 1925. 1925!* Her mind began racing again, that was almost one hundred years ago! How could that be? How could she be a hundred years in the past? Yet there it was right under the name of the newspaper, *The Santa Barbara Daily News.*

She noticed the people here spoke funny, like Americans on the TV shows she watched, but a different kind of American. She wasn't sure what made it different, and wondered if it was just an old-timey way of talking. Or maybe it was how everyone in this place talked. The way people from her country talked mostly alike.

Where was Santa Barbara, anyway? She had never heard of it. She knew the towns around the farm: Tooley-buc, Swan Hill, Piangil, Nyah West, Goodnight, Mildura, but no Santa Barbara.

She started peppering Ava with questions. "Ava, where is this place?"

"America, in California in a seaside town," Ava explained, "and that's not the strangest thing—"

Ivy broke in excitedly, "Is it really a hundred years ago since we left the farm, a hundred years in the past?"

"Yes, Ivy, at least a hundred years from our time! I have been here nearly seventy years, since when this town was much smaller. Seventy years…" she trailed off.

Ivy paused for a moment, turning to look at Ava. "How could you have been here seventy years? You look just the same as yesterday," she protested.

"I don't know, I just never got old like all the other people, like Adeline. She was my age when I came here, now she is a very old lady. It gets even stranger, Ivy, there are so many things to tell you."

Ivy continued on with her questioning, starting to talk faster. "How did you know this place was here?"

"I didn't! I was on the ring tree and a bird sat right next to me and told me to jump off and I did. Well, he didn't speak, but I knew what he meant. I was so tired, so sad. I didn't know what was going to happen but I knew something strange would happen, I just knew it. I wanted to get away, but I didn't know it would be so long until you joined me. It took so long…" Again, Ava trailed off as they continued up the street of the old-timey town.

"Did you see the stars zooming past? Did you see them?" Ivy asked.

"Yes! I saw them too! I'll never forget them. So fast, I could hardly see, then next thing I know I was sitting under that tree back there and Adeline was there and I almost killed her with fright. I thought she was crazy, now I know she's not. We're not the first to come here, Ivy, there are others."

"From our time, from the farm?" Ivy asked.

"Yes, a few. Norah is here and her daughter. I live with them. They came before me. There are others, too, not just from the farm but from all over. Some say they are from times in the future, like space men. I don't know how many are here but they're from all over."

Ivy walked beside her friend, looking around at this strange and beautiful town, hearing snippets of conversations from people passing by, but still not understanding how all this could be happening.

Ava continued. "Some come from long ago and far-off places. I've seen people from Australia from the time before our people got there. I saw original American people before the white people came here. Seems like this is a gathering place, people from all over the world and all over time come here on their way to somewhere else or just stay for a while and go home," she said with a big sigh.

"But how does all this work, Ava? And why did you leave me?" Ivy asked in a desperate tone.

"I've been here so long and I still don't know how it all works. Too long, actually. There are people here that don't like me and Norah and Sharron." She paused with a quizzical expression. "Some are calling us witches now.

It's because we don't get old, and people have noticed and they're calling us witches and want us to go."

Ava glanced around then continued a little faster and softer, as if to stop people from listening. "I made them stay, Ivy, until you came. I wasn't sure if I could get back and I knew you would come, I just didn't know how long."

Ava sounded sad again. It seemed to Ivy that all that time was too long to wait. Too long for a best friend, a cousin, even, to wait. But Ava had waited a whole lifetime for her, and thinking of it made Ivy sad too. She did not know how that must feel, but thought it must be awfully lonely.

Ivy loved Ava like no other person, but she wondered if she could wait that long for her to come back. Even though she knew that without Ava she would not even want to be a person, that the two of them were like one person, she felt seventy years was a long, long time.

"How did you do it, Ava? How did you wait so long?" At first, Ivy was not sure she had said it out loud.

"I didn't know how long it would be. I just waited one day and then the next. When you didn't come for so many years, I thought maybe I was crazy and the farm life wasn't real. But a deeper part of me knew it was real, so I just kept waiting. I started meeting the other people, the people from the other places, and that helped me remember that the farm was real and you were real, so I just waited. Then Norah and Sharron became my family and we all waited for you to come and be part of a family here."

"When did Norah get here?" Ivy asked with head tilted. "Norah was from way before our time," she continued as if thinking to herself.

"She said just before me, like hours before me," Ava said.

As Ivy was trying to get her head around all Ava was saying, they turned a corner and came across a giant building, much taller than anything around it. The big, beautiful building had a big sign that read "Granada Theater."

Ava saw Ivy staring at it. "That's a special place, Ivy! Maybe as special as the tree. They built it last year and all sorts of famous people come to perform there. But sometimes people from far away times go into that building and don't come out," Ava explained.

She stared up at it as she went on. "There's something about this place, this whole place," and with this she spread her arms out, "something magical, I guess. But some people here are scared of it, the ones who think we are witches," she said quietly, and picked up her pace, as though just saying the words made her a little scared.

"We'll come back and look at it later, Ivy. Let's go to the shed and see Norah and Sharron. They'll be so excited to meet you, and you have someone else to meet too!"

They rounded the next corner and were greeted by a man who tipped his hat. "Hola Ava, que paso?" he said. *Hello, Ava, what's up?*

"Estoy bien, Edwardo, pero muy ocupado. ¡Voy a verte pronto!" Ava responded. *I'm well, Edward, but very busy. I'm in a hurry!*

"What language are you talking? When did you learn that? What were you saying?" Ivy inquired as they moved faster up the street.

"Spanish. Lots of people here speak Spanish. This used to be Spain and then Mexico, now America, and before that it was native peoples, like on the farm, before the white people came. So I learned Spanish, " Ava said as she moved to the other side of the street. "I was just saying hello to my friend who lives up here and runs a *tienda*, I mean shop. He's one of the good ones, you can trust him. He came from far away like us, but you can't trust everyone, some of the people are getting mean."

Ava stopped in front of a big tall building that smelled kind of bad to Ivy. Ava pushed open a door and led her into the shed. Inside were horses, lots of horses, old and young, big and small.

"These are my horses! Well, the horses we care for. We get to live here if we look after them. I gave them all names and they all like us. I tell Norah we are a horse family and they are our kids!" Ava giggled and took Ivy to the back of the shed.

There was a set of stairs leading up to a loft full of hay. As they got to the top, Ivy saw them, plain as day in the light streaming through the window. Sitting in front of her was the lady and child from the picture. Shocked, Ivy stumbled back into a hay bale.

THE SHED
ON THE HILL

I vy tried to collect herself. She knew it was Norah with her long flowing hair and the pretty but sad face. Next to her was the girl, maybe two or three years old, just like in the picture. Darker skinned, hair all a mess, and wearing a big smile.

"This is Ivy, Norah, I told you she would come, I told you!" Ava blurted out.

"Welcome, Ivy, we are so excited to meet you after all this time! I was sure she would come, Ava, but it certainly has been a long time. You two have a very special friendship and not even time can stop it. I knew that when I first met you."

Norah smiled at Ivy and looked down at her little girl. "Say hello, Sharron, this is Ava's friend Ivy from the farm!"

"Hello, Ivy," the little girl replied, her small voice filled with excitement. "Did you see all the horsies, Ivy? We have lots of horsies!" Sharron moved closer to Ivy as she knelt down to meet her.

Norah stood behind Sharron, and without knowing it, had put her hand on Ivy's shoulder, filled with awe and tears. This girl was real, this whole thing was real, and the love Norah had for Ava she now instantly shared with her cousin and lifelong, lost and dearest friend in front of her.

Norah knew something of life and friendship, but for Ava and Ivy she felt the kind of love a mother felt for a child, like she felt about Sharron. It made the wait all the more sweet and impossible to fathom.

"I did! They are beautiful horses, Sharron," Ivy said, surprised by her own ability to talk, with all that was happening. But the little girl made her feel safe. Everything about her was lovely, even if Ivy found the moment so strange.

"Mumma, can I show her the horsies? Can I please show them to Ivy?" the girl pleaded. It was clear to Sharron that Ivy was already a friend and must be shown all the horses immediately.

"Yes, but not just yet, Sharron. We have to tell Ivy about some of our secrets and how this place all works. Why don't you go feed Skipper some hay?" Norah handed Sharron a stock of hay and in an instant the little girl was gone down the stairs, apparently to perform a favorite task.

Norah then turned to Ivy and embraced her with a hug so hard and long that Ivy thought she might disappear inside this woman's heart.

"I expect you have some questions. I expect you have a lot," Norah said, finally letting her go.

Ivy took a deep breath and turned to Ava and grabbed her hand, just as Ava had done to her. "I have so many questions, my brain feels like it might explode! How did I get here? How did we all get here?" she asked with earnest sincerity.

"Oh, Ivy, I wish I knew. I can tell you what we know, but what we don't know is much more," Norah replied. "It seems like this place is a kind of intersection, a place where people from all over travel to get away from things, usually bad things. A place they rest before going back to where they came from and sometimes to other times and places. Seems like this has been happening a long time."

"How long...and how did you know?" Ivy asked.

"The people before us said this has been happening from before they even got here. The old ones tell of other people, dark people, coming from faraway places and staying for a time, then returning. They marked the places where this would happen. Marked them rocks and stories," Norah continued

"And with trees?" Ivy blurted out.

"Yes, with trees, like on the farm back in Australia. They would mark them with ring trees, these special places. The holes, I call them. The holes through time," Norah explained.

Ava chimed in. "They made the ring trees when they were just tiny things and bound the little limbs together.

They planted the trees right near these holes in time, and as the trees grew, the rings would grow and mark the spot."

"How many are there? What are they?" Ivy asked quickly, trying to find out all she could as if time was now a precious thing that could not be wasted.

"In some places they would mark these holes with small piles of rocks. In other places with *giant* rocks, like in England and a place called Easter Island. In each place it is the same though. The thing marks the spot where the holes in time are, and people travel through those holes," Norah continued.

"But why and how, how does this all work?" Ivy continued with her anxious questioning.

"Not everyone can go through the holes, and I have not worked that part out. Seems like the people that can must have a good reason, or be very sad and need to come and rest," Norah said.

Ivy sat on a hay bale with a thump, still holding Ava's hand, transfixed.

Norah continued. "We are still trying to work out the rules, Ivy. There seem to be rules. Perhaps the strangest one is that girls and women don't grow old here, but boys and men do."

Ivy glanced at Ava quickly, as if to confirm she had indeed stayed as young as Ivy.

Norah kept on. "Boys that stay too long turn into men and men that stay too long grow old, but not the girls. Sharron is three, and has been three all these years.

Maybe over seventy years now. Never grew older, neither did I or Ava, we are the same age as when we got here."

Suddenly, from around a big hay bale came an old man, moving slowly and giving Ivy such a fright. Looking closer at him, Ivy thought maybe she knew him. But how could she know an old man in this strange place, from this time?

"The boys grow old, Ivy. I grew old," he said softly.

Hearing his voice, Ivy knew she was right. She did know who this was! She got up slowly, and for the first time, let go of Ava's hand. She walked up to the old man, staring at him, and reached out her hand to touch his arm. "Brett, is that you?'' she asked in a tiny, soft voice.

"Yes, it is me. I have missed you. You look just the same, just exactly the same," he said as tears welled up in his eyes. "I have missed you so…" he said again.

Ivy continued, awestruck by the strangeness of it all. "But how did you get here? You drowned, you didn't come though the ring tree!" she asked desperately.

Brett looked at Norah, who seemed to know more about such things.

"The ring trees mark some of the places, Ivy, they don't seem to be all the holes. There are others. Maybe the markers got buried or flooded by the river. Maybe there are some ring trees down under the river now marking places from long ago," Norah suggested.

"I found one!" Ivy exclaimed with realization. "I went right through one, it was in one of the hollow trees by the river. Only it didn't bring me here, it took me to the ring tree!"

"Oh my!" Norah responded. "We don't hear about that much, but that is not the first time. A few people here say some of the holes appear to be bridges to other holes in the same time."

Norah looked off as if trying to put together a puzzle that was a little too difficult for her to finish.

Ivy turned back to Brett. "How old are you now? What have you been doing all these years?"

Brett looked right at her. "I guess I am in my eighties It sure feels like it," he said with the same old cheeky smile of his youth.

"But you died. You never came up and everyone thought we must have killed you, they never found your body..." Ivy slowed down realizing what she was saying. "Of course, you didn't die. You came here, you came from under the water!"

He nodded at her realization. "I have been doing odd jobs, mostly helping Norah and Ava and Sharron make a life here. And waiting for you, Ivy. We all waited for you because we did not know what else to do. Ava wanted to get the old team back together and here we are." Brett smiled a wry smile.

The boy was still in the man, Ivy could see. That mischievous boy still lived behind that wrinkled face after all these years. That boy she had not stopped thinking about every day since he was gone.

"Did you see my father before you left, Ivy? I wonder about him sometimes," Brett asked.

"No, I left right after Ava and I did not see him. I never really saw him before you left, but he must miss you," Ivy said, staring at Brett again.

"Oh, I don't think so. From what I recall, he did not really notice me so much, that's why I spent all my time with you and Ava," Brett said sadly. "Not sure he would notice, not much of a family, that one. But you know what? I made a new family right here with Norah and Ava and Sharron. We've been a family for a long time, now. But it is strange that I am like the grandpa and they are all still so young. Sharron thinks I am her grandpa and that's fine with me. Makes me feel needed in these last days, Ivy, makes me feel…" he trailed off, then finished, "makes me feel loved."

Another tear rolled down his cheek as Norah touched his hand, leaned over and kissed his head. "Our dear grandpa," she said so softly and tenderly. "We do all so love you, Brett, for helping us stay safe all these years. Always so kind, so full of mischief and fun. First as a boy, then a man, now a grandpa," Norah said as she turned back to Ivy with her eyes full of love and tears.

Norah noticed a look on Brett's face, she had seen it before, and she recognized it again now as he looked at her. She knew something about that look and what it meant. She knew Brett's secret and had kept it all these years. Brett loved Ivy, had all his life, this one and the one before. He had loved her when they were kids and loved her as he waited all these years, and he loved her even now as an old man. Norah knew this and she understood.

Sure, Brett had girlfriends, when he was young and as he got older. Despite this, Brett had told Norah his secret many years ago when she asked him why he did not try to go back to his time. He told her that he loved Ivy and would wait with Ava until she came. He could not risk missing her and going back to the farm without her there. He had loved some of these other people, but they were not Ivy, so he waited for her.

Here he was, all these years later, all that waiting and here was Ivy. Norah saw in that moment that he still loved this girl and despite his age, he still loved her just like he did when he was just a boy himself. It was a curious thing to Norah who had now lived so long. This kind of love usually happened later in life, but here was a kid who had become an old man and had loved the same girl for his entire life.

Norah was both sad and happy at the same time, the happy-sad place that they all knew. Happy that Brett got to be with Ivy again, sad that for Brett it had taken a lifetime.

Family, Stories,
and Horses

"Do you remember when we all first met, Ava?" Brett was sitting on a log in the shed full of horses and chewing the dried beef that he loved so much. On one end of the shed was a hay loft, and one of his jobs was to throw the bales up into the loft, and since the girls were not strong enough, he did it all himself. All that exercise, and probably all that beef jerky, had made him "strong as a horse," Ava had often said, and Sharron would always laugh. Even now, as an old man, the muscles on his arms were large and chiseled from years of heavy lifting.

"Of course, I remember! We've talked about it many times," Ava said, but not in the least bit irritated as she loved to remember it and now it was time for Ivy to hear. "I had just arrived the day before and Adeline told me there was another kid in town that talked just like me and

I should meet him. She didn't know where he came from but she knew he had just arrived."

Ava looked at Brett as he tugged on the dry meat. Sharron had returned and now sat between them, listening intensely as she always did when they told their stories.

"Adeline and I started walking through the town, just looking around and trying to find the new kid in town with the funny accent," Ava continued. "Then down by the creek we heard a noise, a voice, down on the banks."

At this, Sharron jumped in. "I know! I know what he said!" She turned to Norah who was sitting on a log fixing a hole in one of Sharron's skirts. "Can I say it, Mumma?" she asked Norah.

"Yes, you can, but remember it is a bad word. But for the sake of the story, with us, you can say it." Norah half smiled at Sharron.

With that, Sharron put on her very best Australian accent and with her squeaky little voice said, "Got you, you little bastard!" She fell over and started giggling. She did not know what a little bastard was but she knew it was naughty and it made her giggle every time.

"That's right, Sharron, and we looked down over the bank and there was this kid all covered in mud, head to toe, holding a fish trying its very best to jump out of his hands and get back into the creek," Ava remembered.

Ivy grinned at Brett, picturing him covered in mud as she had seen him many times playing near the river.

"And right next to that kid was another kid, a young, darker-skinned kid also covered in mud and laughing so hard we thought he might faint," Ava said while Sharron let out even more giggles at the thought of it.

Ava said with a huge grin at the remembrance of it, "Adeline called down to them and asked them if they caught a fish or if the fish had caught them. Then both boys looked up, one Chumash and one, well the other one, at first, we couldn't tell what he looked like since he was completely covered in mud. He looked up, and when he saw us, he dropped the fish right back into the water and stared like he had seen a ghost."

She continued now but in a quieter voice. "Then I realized why he had dropped the fish and turned to stone. I did the same thing when I realized the new kid with the funny accent was you, Brett. You had come back from the dead." Ava let out a kind of snorting sound, like a sob.

Brett took over the story now, almost in a trance. "We recognized each other through the mud, through the strangeness of the place that had a river, but it was not our river. I think we both thought we might just be dreaming. I remember stuttering, 'Ava... Ava, is that you?'"

"And I told him yes and ran right down that bank, but before I got to him, I tripped and landed face-first in the mud!" Ava smiled and Sharron again burst out giggling. "Brett, you came right over to me and picked me up, and wiped the mud off my face and kept saying 'Ava, Ava is that you? Where are we, how did you get here?'"

Ava started to laugh. "And you know what, Brett? It's the same thing we keep saying to ourselves every day we've been here: 'Is that you and where are we?'"

Ivy chimed in, "That's what I've been saying since I landed in that tree!"

The trance now broken, they all laughed, laughed at the scene, at the fish and the mud and then, as always, came the sadness. Sadness that the young boy helping Brett find a fish to eat was one of the many friends they made in those first few months that had died so soon after. So many of the first people of that land had died, were dying, and would die soon. It was a sad and confusing time.

"What happened to him, the boy with at the river, Brett?" Ivy asked.

Norah said that she thought that as the new people were coming to the West, they brought disease with them from the old world that these people had never had and they got sick and died.

"I still miss our old friend, Ava, there are so few of the first people left now," Brett said quietly and had stopped chewing on his meat. Then he brightened. "I was so shocked to see you, so happy, I thought I had gone crazy or would go crazy but with you here, at least I wouldn't go crazy alone. One moment I'm on the farm swimming in the river, the next I'm in this place, then you show up! And strangest of all, you show up without Ivy! I'd never seen you two apart but there you were and she was not…"

Brett tried to hide it but there was something like a pain in the saying of it out loud.

"I was so confused, Brett, but I've never been so happy to see someone from home, ever. Even if that person was a dead person!" Ava laughed and the rest all joined in.

"Then I met you both, the strangest thing of all for me, I think." Norah was speaking now. "I had gotten here before you, not too long. And I had made our room right here in the shed with the horses."

Ava and Brett nodded, as Norah went on, recalling how their little family found each other.

"At some point, we all realized we were from the same farm in Australia, but I was there so many years before, you were not even born when I lived on the river. Then we show up in this place right around the same time..." Norah trailed off, the same old wonder in her voice. "I am not sure we will ever know how this all works, but I'm so glad we're here together. Who else would believe this crazy story?" She looked at them all with a wide and beautiful grin.

"We talked about you so much, Ivy. We wondered how to get home and be with you again," Brett said. "We've wondered all these years if you would come, and now you're here."

He smiled as he looked at Ivy, and she smiled back at him with a precious smile that came from deep in her heart.

THE LIE

In the years before Ivy arrived, there were many nights when they sat at the end of the day and talked about how they had all met, how they had all ended up in this strange and wonderful place together. Not once did these nights end without someone asking if they thought Ivy would come soon.

More and more often, however, the discussion turned to trying to find a way back. As each year passed, the place they found themselves in got a little stranger. It was, of course, some time ago when they realized that Ava and Norah were not getting older, yet Brett was. That is not to say they were not all changing on the inside. Life was happening to all of them and life changes you. Sharron had changed the least, though, as she seemed to be much the same, she did seem to know much more than her age would suggest and understand much more than girls her age.

Ava, while she looked the same, had changed the most. On the outside she was just a young woman, barely past being a young girl herself, but on the inside she was changing with the times. But it was a deeper kind of change, caused by more than things like watching all the events of the town. It was watching friends come and go. Watching friends grow old and die, and some never getting the chance to grow old, and just dying. These were the things that really changed Ava.

There was not a day that went by that Ava didn't wonder why she was not aging, at least on the outside. There was a lady once, at a funeral Ava went to, that made her think a strange thought. Over the casket of one of the Brooks' boys who had drowned in the ocean while building the new wharf, she said the strangest thing that stayed with Ava. She said that Jimmy Brooks, now cold and dead and ready to be buried in the ground, would be "forever young." Forever young! A young person that died never had to grow old, they would be forever young.

Maybe, Ava thought, she was actually dead and would be forever young! Because, like Jimmy Brooks, she was actually already dead. Brett was growing old, so maybe he was not already dead and therefore, growing old. The idea that she might be dead now stayed with her, and seemed to make a lot of sense. She was, according to this theory, dead, and so were Norah and Sharron. Only Brett was not dead in this place; he was just growing old like a normal alive person.

It made her head ache sometimes thinking about it.

One beautiful day in the town, full of light and excitement and activity, Ava, Sharron, and Norah had decided to take a walk down by the new pier that had recently been built to service the ships that seemed to be growing in number every day coming to the town. The pier had become known as "Stearns Wharf" after the man that started the project some years before.

Ava loved coming down to the beach, it was big, so beautiful, and she often looked out over it and thought of the farm on the other side so far away, and strangely, so far off in the future. There were clouds out in the distance, grey and black, and the wind was picking up. A storm was coming so they had decided to make their way back to the shed before it arrived.

As they turned on the beach a woman looked up and stared at them. "Ava, is that you?" she asked in a fierce kind of tone.

At first Ava was going to lie, but this was not the first time this had happened, and she had come up with an answer she used a few times that mostly seemed to work.

"Yes, yes," she said, "Is that you, Anna?" Ava said cautiously.

Ava knew who this was, it was a girl that years ago had lived in this town and she was not very nice, to say the least. She often teased Ava and made fun of the way she talked. She rallied some of the other girls around her to do the same. Ava never knew why she picked on her, she had never done anything to this girl.

Norah had a theory that she shared with Ava one night when the teasing had made Ava so sad and then so very angry. "I think," Norah had suggested, "it is because you are so beautiful, Ava."

Ava was shocked by this, she had never been called beautiful before and even if she was, why would that be the reason to tease her so relentlessly?

"Ava, you are quite shockingly beautiful for a girl your age, and Anna was *the* pretty young girl in town before you arrived. Everyone told her so, and all the boys noticed her and gave her lots of attention."

Norah went on. "Then along you came, and all the eyes and attention moved to you and away from her. I know you didn't notice and still don't because you are in another place in your head, but you are a beauty, and everyone but you knows it. I think Anna is very jealous of you and all the attention you took from her."

"But I didn't do anything! Why would that make her so mean?" Ava said but she knew why. She was old enough to know about such things as jealousy and the things it could make you do.

There was once a boy in school that Ava thought was different from the other boys and they had become friends. She thought this boy might be more than just a friend, that he might be the first boy she would kiss. She liked him so much, she even decided that this kiss would happen at the school social the following week, where everyone had their first kiss at her school. At least, it seemed that way from all the older girls talking about it in the yard. These social events happened at night in the school hall, there was music and dancing and darkness. The teachers patrolled the area to make sure the kids were not wandering off to do their kissing and their drinking from stolen bottles of beer, but hiding places were easy to find.

On this night, Ava could not find this boy she wanted to kiss but had an idea of where he might be. So she quietly slipped out from the hall, around the back of the building and to the group of trees that kids called "lovers' lane." Sure enough, there were some couples "sucking each other's faces," as the boys called it.

Then she saw him, with Jenny of all people. He was kissing Jenny! She was not even in their class, Jenny was a year younger than them. Ava felt her cheeks explode with heat and fire, she was so sad and angry, but mostly she felt stupid and embarrassed.

She slipped out of lovers' lane and never spoke of what she had seen. She never looked at that boy the same way again. Whenever she saw Jenny, a girl she had never really thought too much about, she had that feeling. That feeling that this girl had taken something from her and it could not be given back. She did not hate Jenny, but she never spoke with her or the boy again.

Over time, she knew this was silly and meant to make it right. However, the boy had become a man and died from pneumonia and Jenny had long moved away. She had felt much guilt about it over the years but had learned to forgive herself for just being young and silly.

Ava thought about that story from her past and understood what Norah was telling her, what Anna must have been feeling toward her. That sad jealous thing that could easily turn to hate, when it was never the other person's fault at all. But hate was better than jealousy and sadness, so some people chose that instead.

As memories of that talk with Norah flooded back to Ava standing on the beach, Anna spoke again. "My Lord in heaven, Ava, you look the same! Look at you, you never grew up! I have been gone from this town fifteen years and yet you still look the same. Not a wrinkle, not a thing has changed." Anna said it in the same angry tone of all those years ago.

She then turned to the people with her and started ranting. "I know this girl from when I lived here! We're the same age, but look at her, she hasn't changed one bit! How can that be? How can she be the same all these years later?" Anna spouted out the words and the people with her looked shocked and concerned.

Ava quickly launched into her explanation as she knew where this could go and it was dangerous. "I'm sick, Jenny! I have a disease, they don't know what causes it, but I am *really* sick. I'm getting very old very fast on the inside, but on the outside I look the same." She used her best acting voice, sounding so very sad.

Then she added, for dramatic effect, "They say I'll die real soon. On the inside my body is all old and dying, and the cruel part is that I still look so young on the outside."

This seemed not only to work but to actually delight Anna. "Oh my! I am so sorry to hear that, Ava, we were such good friends," she said but could not hide the grin turning her mouth up at the sides. Others may have missed it, but to Ava it was clear as day. She knew that look, she felt that hate coming from Anna.

"That is so sad, Ava. When do they think you will die?" Anna went on in her fake sad voice.

"Could be any week now, they say," Ava replied as Norah moved to her side and put her hand on Ava's shoulder in a show of mock sadness. Sharron hid behind her mother's dress so as not to be seen, as Norah had told her to do. Norah understood this little plan of Ava's could only work so well. If people in the town started to notice, really notice, that Ava was not aging it could be extremely dangerous to stay longer.

Anna was just one of the people amazed that Ava was apparently not aging. More and more people were beginning to notice, and since they didn't understand it, they were suspicious of Ava. It wouldn't be long, Norah feared, before they came after her, demanding she explain herself—or worse, punish her for being different. It was indeed getting dangerous to stay in this place.

Little Traveler and the Rescue

Standing there on the beach, one moment Ava's brain was focused on trying to divert this woman from the obvious bizarre fact that she had not aged. This Anna, now older and no doubt more powerful in her world, could do Ava real damage and would delight in it. All those thoughts, all that brain activity about what to say and how to diffuse the threat, immediately evaporated the instant Ava became aware of the chaos mounting all around them at the beach.

The winds had started to really pick up. Suddenly, they heard shouts and saw that a ship full of Chinese workers had apparently crashed hard into the wharf. Men were thrown overboard and could now be seen scrambling in the water for their lives. It was a scene of complete chaos. Men screaming and thrashing about in the water, waves and wood crashing. In an instant, Ava took off and ran toward the water without another thought.

It was a reflex, an overwhelming instinct. People were in trouble, drowning, and her situation was no longer important to her, helping others was all that mattered. It was who she was, it was what she had become. Yet it all happened without a conscious thought.

All those years living by the ocean had changed Ava's relationship to water. On the farm there was fear, dread, and loss associated with water. Here, Ava had learned to love it. For years, every day she swam, hot or cold, high surf or no surf. This was her place now and she had become an exceptional swimmer. She could literally swim for miles and hold her breath for many minutes at a time. The sea creatures had become like the horses, more than pets, more than unknowable beasts, they were friends, part of the world she inhabited.

She sprinted to the wharf, all the while assessing the situation. The boat, a strange looking one in her mind, had mis-timed its docking and with a rising surf, slammed into the pier as the men aboard were preparing to disembark. Many of these men had probably come to work on projects like the making of this dock and the new railway. They were Chinese and had come from thousands of miles away.

So many Chinese were building out this new land with blood, sweat, tears, and often their lives. She had met some in her time here, good hard-working people trying to make some money for families back home in this new and strange land. This would be the story of America for many years to come. Hard-working people looking for a new start, new work, with an eye to sending money home to family they may never see again.

Ava found these stories much like her own. People far away in a strange land hoping to return home to the land of their youth, but not knowing if that would ever happen. The difference was, in their case it was by choice. They were the brave ones, she had just appeared, but they chose to come. Their bravery apparently made her brave as she continued to race to the wharf at full speed.

Most of the men, and they were mostly men, had scrambled to find logs to hang onto and some were even making their way to the beach. Some, however, were failing, splashing, clearly not knowing how to swim.

Ava picked one out, a young man not much older than her, desperately trying to stay above the water. She sprinted to the part of the wharf that was still standing and launched herself off the edge into the air with such grace and speed that those that saw it thought she might simply fly away. She hit the water ten feet from the man and dove underneath it behind him. He was tiring now, and she had seen this before. The drowning panic, cannot be spoken too, and in this case, might not even speak the language.

Ava knew she had to take control from behind, had to avoid the punches and kicks that come from the dying's last hope of holding on. As she emerged, she saw what she needed: a log big enough to float this man, a piece of wood broken free from the wharf or the boat.

She grabbed the log, put it in front of her, and pushed it at full speed behind the man. In one quick movement, she wedged the log between herself and the man, at the same time reaching under his arms to pick him up. At first, he resisted, confused, but he was too weak now to put up much of a fight. He soon realized this was a rescue as his head was now above water, with Ava holding him up against the log. He coughed and sputtered but started to get his breath back.

Ava saw another man off the boat's edge trying to get back in, tiring and unable to make it up. With another quick move, she spun the first man around so he could hold onto the log and set her free. He clutched the log with all his might and his head stayed above the water. As Ava pushed off, he looked at her with a mix of terror, relief, and wonder. And also of something like thanks. Ava marveled at how one's eyes could tell so many emotions at once. The eyes indeed being the window to the soul, but also the universal language of the emotions inside.

She did not dwell on the thought or the moment, in an instant she was gone and powering through the water to the man by the boat's edge. He was trying to get onto the deck but it was too high and the side of the boat a little too slippery and wet to hold onto. She could see he was trying to "jump" out of the water but each time it was a little less successful, a little weaker.

She waited for just the right moment and learned his cadence. She then dove under the water, and with perfect timing, swam upward toward him as he made his next feeble attempt. This time, however, as he pushed the water with his legs, they met resistance. He pushed up from this unseen ground with enough force to make it to the deck. He then collapsed and gasped, too exhausted to know that the ground was a young girl that had helped him. Ava had managed to time her ascent perfectly and used herself as a lever for the man to push down on, giving him just enough momentum to make the deck.

For her efforts she was pushed down into the sea, but for her this was no problem. She made a few strides and popped out of the water to see if anyone else needed help. She saw out of the corner of her eye an old friend, Juan, trying to throw a rope from the wharf to a man starting to drift further away from the beach. But Juan, old now and not the strong man she had met years ago, could not send the rope out far enough to reach him.

Ava raced through the water between Juan and the man floating away. "Juan, tírame la cuerda!" she yelled. *Throw the rope to me!*

Juan threw the rope and it landed short of Ava, but she swam for it and turned and headed out toward the man that was now even farther away. She swam with one arm paddling at full speed and legs working at a furious pace. She reached him and again dove under the water. In a blur of motion, she wrapped the rope under the man's arms, tied it, then burst through the water and yelled to Juan who was now shoulder-to-shoulder with another man.

"Tira la cuerda hacia adentro, está atado!" Ava yelled up at Juan. *Pull the rope in, he is attached!*

Juan and the other man pulled on the rope and off shot the man in the water toward the safety of the wharf. Ava looked around and saw that there was no one left in the water. The ship had not sunk, but like the wharf, it was damaged and would need weeks to repair.

She soon realized she was being pulled out and across the water by a strong rip tide that the man had been caught in, created by the storm. These rip tides were too strong to beat, and would easily drown the strongest of all swimmers if you tried to fight against them. She knew this from experience and from the people that had taught her to swim in the ocean all those years ago. *You don't swim into them, you swim across them*, they had told her, and she did.

Eventually, the rip tide gave up on her and let her free. She was much farther down the beach now, the wharf and the boat in the distance. She was tired but more than up to the task of swimming back to the shore.

As the confusion and panic settled, the people on the wharf had already started talking about the "fish girl" that had saved tens of men. "She flew like a bird and swam like a dolphin!" Each telling of it became more absurd, but this was the way of legend. Each telling made it a little more heroic, a little less of the truth, and absolutely a little more fun and amazing.

Ava did not want, certainly did not need, this attention, and thankfully almost no one knew it was her. She had been too far away to have her exploits seen by Ana and those in the town growing more interested and concerned about her. It was too confusing a situation for the people on the wharf to see a lone girl in the water. Except for one.

An elderly man sat on the wharf, exhausted from helping pull in a drowning man on a rope. The man had survived and Juan was exhausted. Under his breath he spoke to himself, "Ava, eres una maravilla. Tu secreto está a salvo conmigo. Eres un pequeño viajero increíble." *Ava, you are a wonder. Your secret is safe with me. You are an amazing little traveler.*

ALBERT

Not all of Ava's adventures were so dangerous and exciting. Some were more mundane but not less important. Years after the crash at the wharf she met a most extraordinary man on a bicycle whose name was Albert. She had been walking and thinking, which is what she did more and more these days. Thinking about Ivy, thinking about this place, her home back in Australia, and all that had happened. She could not stop thinking about *how* it had happened. How she had turned up in this town, how such a thing as this was possible.

On this day, as she walked alone in the town, a town now much bigger than when she arrived, she saw a man on a bicycle. He stood out to her because of the bike, which always made her think of home, but even more because of his hair. All white and standing straight up, like he'd had a terrible fright and his hair never quite got over it.

She watched him doing circles in the dirt then he looked up and called out to her.

"Hello there, young one! How are you this fine day?"

Immediately, Ava knew this was someone she would like. There was something about this man that was kind and curious and it flowed out of him like a stream.

"I like your bike, sir," she said.

"Yes, indeed, such a marvelous invention! Such a thing to feel like you can go so far and so fast. I will never get tired of just going in circles," he said with a giant grin.

Ava noted he had an accent and was curious to know more. "Where are you from, sir, if I may ask?"

"Germany, but I am thinking of making this country my own. Wonderful place, wonderful people," he said but in a somewhat sad tone. "I am sorry for being rude," he continued as he brightened. "My name is Albert, what is yours?"

"Ava. I live here and I'm pleased to meet you and your bicycle, Mr. Albert. Why are you so far from home?"

"My first name is Albert, but I like the sound or Mr. Albert," he said. "My being here is a long story, Miss Ava, but a friend invited me to come and give some talks, and I fear trouble is brewing in my country, so I thought it best to come and see this place you call America."

"What do you talk about that would make you come so far?" Ava inquired.

"I speak about science and the universe and time and all manner of astrology. I am not so sure I speak very well, but my ideas have had some small effect in the world and so I am asked to come and explain them. But I come to this place just to rest and ride a bike before I go home again," Albert explained.

Ava was immediately fascinated, a scientist that knew about the universe! Might he know how she got here?

"Albert, I have some strange questions I would like to ask. Strange because I'm not sure how the universe works, but maybe you can help me understand," she said shyly.

"Oh, please let us talk! The universe is such a strange place and rarely does one of your age want to speak of such things. I spend all my time thinking about it and it seems to get stranger the more I do. I only seem to talk about it with old men in dark rooms," he said with a great big smile.

"Here is the thing, and it is a big thing, I think. Is it possible to travel back in time and travel over great distances in no time at all without any kind of ship?" Ava asked even more shyly now, knowing her question must sound crazy.

Albert paused, the grin on his face seeming to widen impossibly. "Oh, that is a marvelous question, such a wonderful question. Would it not be marvelous to be able to travel across the universe and back and forth in time? What a marvelous thing that would be, but also, I expect quite dangerous. What things might change if one went back in time, would the whole universe unravel?" He now had a far-off look as if calculating some difficult math question in his head.

"But, do you think it possible?" Ava persisted.

"Well, Miss Ava, it turns out that space and time are all related but not the way they look to us. Did you know that time is not the same everywhere, but can stretch and be different speeds in different places? This is part of my work, you know. The faster you travel the faster time moves in the place you left behind, but not for you. Is that not wonderful?" he asked.

Ava had a sense that some of her questions, a lifetime of questions, might be answered by this man.

Again, Albert had a faraway look as it trying to conjure the entire universe in his head. "I have a colleague that suggests space might have holes and that one could perhaps travel to the other end of the universe in a moment. Like a worm travels through an apple, from one side to the other, instead of having to go all the way around the apple."

This excited Ava greatly as it was very much related to her question. "Albert, can I tell you a story and you tell me if it is possible?" she asked.

"Oh, please, I like to imagine all kinds of things. Do tell me a story," Albert said.

"Is it possible to go from one place to another place and that other place be thousands of miles away and many years in the past?" Ava asked with an intense voice that Albert could see all over her face.

"This is something I have thought very much about, Ava. Space is so strange it can bend, and time with it. I think it is possible to perhaps travel vast distances when space gets bent. I made some equations and calculations about space and time when I was a younger man, and still today I work on them. It is possible that a thing called a black hole might punch through time and space and it might be possible to travel through them at enormous speed to other parts of the universe. The time on one side of the black hole would be experienced very differently from time on the other side," he explained.

He then gave her a cheeky smile. "Of course, it is also possible that going into such a hole might squash you completely and you would be dead and not even know it."

Noticing Ava didn't smile at this, Albert continued more seriously. "I see this is an important question for you, Ava, but my answers are all theory. Theory is where I live. I do not think we will know what is possible for many years."

"Would you think me crazy if I told you this happened to me? That I traveled very far and back in time to come to this place?" Ava said very seriously.

He looked at her a little perplexed, but still with a grin of a wise man. "Well, young Ava, you might well be crazy, that is true, though you certainly do not seem to be. I would say that given what I know of the universe, I think all but a few things may be possible. I have a colleague that has even crazier ideas than mine. His name is Max, and in his universe things can go back and forward in time. He calls it quantum physics, but I do not think God would play games with the universe like this. Honestly, my dear, I do not know," he said looking at her curiously.

Then he asked in a somewhat matter-of-fact manner, like the strangeness of the idea was not that strange to him at all, "Ava when did this thing, this trip, happen and when are you from?"

"I came from the future, and from a far-off place, Australia. I would think that I am completely crazy if not for the fact that I am not the only one. There are others here that have the same story. People I know, and maybe we are all crazy, but our stories are the same. There is some kind of a hole that we have passed through, all light and stars and speed, and at the other end a different place and a different time."

Albert had stopped his bicycle and now stared at her intently. "What do these holes look like? Where are they?" he asked as if trying to picture them.

"I didn't see them, I just kind of fell into one. There was a bird, though, a bird that seemed to be able to see what I could not, and he guided me to it. Then it was like I was out in space moving so very fast, like in a tunnel, and then I was here." Ava looked out into the distance, remembering what had happened so long ago.

"This is so very interesting to me, so very intriguing. I must think about it some more." Albert started to draw in the dirt, making a big circle and then doing calculations that Ava could not understand. He seemed completely lost in thought, in some kind of a trance, like he had moved into a different place in his mind and Ava and this world had been left behind.

After a long time, Ava bid her farewell, telling Albert she had to go but would return tomorrow to talk more. He did not answer but continued his work in the dirt.

Ava did return, but she never saw the man again. She saw a kindly old lady in the place where she and Albert had talked, and she asked her where Albert had gone.

"Oh, he's gone back to Germany. He's a very important man, and he says he is working on some new theories that he started thinking about when talking to a young lady," the old lady said while looking at her curiously. "Are you that girl?"

"Yes, I believe I am," Ava said shyly, like she might get in trouble for it.

"Stay here one moment, he left a note for you." The old woman walked back into the house then returned almost immediately. "He asked me to give this to you if you returned." She handed Ava an envelope with a short note inside.

It read:

Dear Miss Ava,

I have had to return to Germany with great haste. There are people there trying to destroy my great country and put my people at great risk. I must return immediately to see if I can help.

I do not think you are crazy. I think that what you say is possible. I even think you could go back the same way! I have done some calculations and I think that these holes are indeed possible. I will continue to work on these calculations and I hope with all my heart that after these troubles are over, I can come back to this place and meet you and your friends and talk more. You might be the most interesting person I have ever met, Miss Ava.

With great regard and wonder,

Albert Einstein (Mr. Albert)

Ava read it slowly, her heart beating like thunder as she got to the end and realized who her friend "Mr. Albert" really was. She had heard his name in class and in life. Einstein was well, *Einstein!* She had met one of the most famous people in history and one of the world's greatest scientists. The weight of it, the very strange wonderful nature of the thing, took her breath away.

She looked up at the old woman who stood watching her curiously. "When will he return, miss?" she asked pleadingly.

"I do not know. It is a bad time in his country, very bad people are trying to come to rule his country and I do not know when he will be back. He was very taken with you, though. He said he has never met anyone like you and was very sad to have to leave." And with that, the old lady smiled and turned away.

Ava read the note again, as she would many, many times in the years ahead.

The Witches
of Equestrian

After Ava finished telling Ivy of some of her adventures, including the story of Mr. Albert and more, a growing tension began rising in the shed. Despite all that had happened, all the reunions and love in the air, there was a problem and it was now time to make a decision.

"Ava," Norah said in a serious tone as they sat among the hay bales and heard the soft whinnying from the horses below. "I think it is time for us to leave. We have stayed too long and the troubles are starting. Ivy is here now, and it is time to leave."

Ava looked at Norah and with sad but knowing eyes she nodded in agreement.

"Why? What, what troubles, Ava?" Ivy asked, almost pleading.

"Ivy, for a long time we knew this place should only be visited, you should not stay too long here. It is a place to rest, not a place for people from our time, from other times, to live," Ava said.

"We have been here so long," Norah explained, "and the people that live here are getting anxious. Ava has not grown old and people have noticed now, not just Anna. She has to hide more and more."

Brett chimed in. "And worst of all, there's a preacher in town who says the people have lost their way and the devil is coming. Last week he said there are witches in town, warning people of two young girls that live in town who never age. He said they must be witches sent to this place to perform a 'judgment,' whatever that means."

"He is the kind of preacher that blames all the bad things on the devil and witches and then tries to frighten people to come to church and be safe," Norah added.

Ava stood up and started to pace back and forth anxiously. "I've been hiding more and more, trying not to be seen. I read about the Salem Witch trials, Ivy, which happened right here in America. A whole bunch of people got accused of being witches and the townspeople killed them! They hung them, and worse!"

Ivy's eyes grew wide at this, sensing the danger her friends were in.

"I can feel something happening, Ivy, something bad coming. It's time for us to go home. I've stayed much too long, but now that you're here we can try and go back together!" Ava declared.

"She is right, Ivy. Brett and I have been talking about it too." Norah looked over at Brett who nodded solemnly. "Brett wants to go home now, one more time. He's old and it is time."

Brett walked over to Ivy and sat down beside her with a sigh. "It's true, Ivy. We have waited all this time, made a good life here, but this is not a place to stay too long and we have been here too long. I'd like to go back home one more time. To see the river and my home and the farm one more time. I never forgot it. The funny thing is, the older I get the more I think about it. Our times as kids on the farm were the best times, even when they were the worst. Being a kid with you guys, running around the farm, our imag-inations, the wide-open space. They were the best times, Ivy. Why is it that an old man longs for the times when he was just a boy above all the other times in his life..."

He started to trail off then looked over at Ivy, as if remembering where he was. "Now that you're here, we can all go back together."

Norah suddenly looked sad and said, "Except I am not from your time. I am from a time before. I am not sure how this works, but I suspect if we go back, I will go back to my time and you to yours."

She looked around the room at each of them, the real-ization of what she had said dawning in their eyes.

Norah went on, "Back in the beginning, when I first came here, I thought it was wonderful to not grow old and for Sharron to always be a little child. But it ain't right,

Ivy. Little girls should grow up, women should grow old. I have to take her back and we have to live a proper life." She said this with some sadness but also something like relief at the saying of it out loud.

She continued. "I did not want to go back for a very long time, because the people became mean in my time. They called me all kinds of things, horrible things because a sad thing happened and I could not fix it."

Norah was starting to trail off into some distant past in her head, remembering that long time ago. "Back then I was a nurse, living right on the river with my husband. Looked after the river boat people if they needed help and they often did. Then my husband died, drowning right in the river in front of our little shack. Died saving Sharron who had fallen in."

Norah now had tears rolling down her cheeks. "Then a man came and said he wanted to be my husband. He was a bad man, a mean man. He was real bad to us, Ivy, real bad. He started telling people terrible stories about me to keep other people away. Told them I did things I never did. He lied to all the people and he was so mean to us I had to leave."

Sharron scooted closer to her mother and lay her head against her arm, as though comforting her as she told this familiar sad tale.

"So, one night I woke up Sharron and we ran off, not knowing where to go. Strangest thing is, a bird landed on my door and seemed to be guiding me. We waded across the river and ran across the way until I came to the ring tree. I climbed right up it with Sharron, just like you did, not even sure why. The bird came right along with us, as though it was asking us to go there. Then Sharron fell right off the tree and was gone. Slipped right off, I think, but it looked like she jumped. I jumped right after her to catch her and we ended up here. Right where the big tree is now in town. Ended up right there," Norah repeated as if the story now was a memory of a memory as old memories can be.

Ivy listened with her whole body. She could almost feel it again, that jump-fall into the unknown below.

Norah sighed and shook her head, as if coming out of a trance. "Made a new life here, meeting Brett and Ava, and we waited for you, Ivy. But now a storm is coming and we can feel it getting closer. Sharron needs to grow up. Ain't right to keep her a child forever..."

Norah looked much older than she did just a few minutes before. There was a weariness to her, but a determination. Ivy could see it, they all could see it.

"How do we go home? How does that work?" Ivy asked no one in particular.

"Let's go see the old lady," Norah said. "Up at the mission, I heard she is back. She comes and goes to this place and stays at the mission."

"She's the one who told us to not stay too long. But we did and I agree with Norah, it's time to go," Ava added.

Brett turned to Ivy and explained further. "She's an old Chumash lady. Said she came from the past, when it was just Chumash here and no people from the 'big boats' as she called them. She says she comes to get medicine for her people from her time. She's like a healer or a doctor or…"

"Like me, some kind of nurse," Norah finished for him. "She found a way here by accident too, right up by the old mission. Said the first time she came the nuns thought she was a ghost, just showed right up in the mission and scared them half to death!"

"They treated her like some kind of a spirit," Ava said. "She's a very old lady and she doesn't stay too long. She only comes for a few days and goes right back. Just long enough to collect some things before going back."

Norah stood up and stated resolutely, "Let's go right now and see her, she'll know what to do. She's the one to ask."

With that, Ivy, Ava, and Norah headed out from the shed while Brett and Sharron stayed behind. Going out was a risk, but they needed to go fast and Brett was old and Sharron was just a kid, so they stayed and fed the horses. Ava had wrapped herself in a head scarf to try and hide a little, as did Norah.

People had started to talk about them. Some said their parents and even grandparents knew Ava and Norah and Sharron from many years ago. Something was not right, they said, so they had taken to hiding as best they could.

They donned their clothes and scarves and headed up to the mission.

"What is the mission, anyway?" Ivy asked Norah as they walked.

Norah took a breath as if forming her thoughts and words. "The mission was built by the Spaniards in 1786, they say. They built a bunch of them up and down the coast so they could travel a day between them and then rest."

"What people? Who owns them?" Ivy asked.

"The Spanish. They brought nuns and padres and missionaries who tried to convert the first peoples to the Spanish king's religion."

Ivy glanced over at Norah, who seemed saddened by this.

Norah went on. "The old Chumash lady said lots of people died. Got sick from the Spanish and died. Others moved away, some stayed. Then the Spanish left and this place became Mexico, then there was a war and it became America. All that time, the mission stayed, and the old lady would visit from time to time to get her medicine and tell her stories and then go back."

Norah took another breath. She knew she had said this many times, but the saying of it made her feel less anxious: "She is the one that will know what to do. I am sure of it."

"Can we come back here, Norah? Can we see you again if we go back"? Ava asked.

She was suddenly sad, as if after all these years this was the first time she had thought that Norah would go back to another time and they would not be together. Norah had become Ava's mother, in a way, they had lived a long time together as a family. How would it be without her new family? Ava felt sad and a little frightened at the thought of it, even though she herself was the age of an old woman, inside she still felt like a kid. Maybe we all do for all time, she thought.

They turned the corner and Ivy gave out a little noise. "I know this place!" she announced, speaking fast and excitedly. "I have seen this place! Ava, I saw it in a picture of you and Norah and Sharron and Brett, right here. The picture was at Norah's place, right on the floor, I found it!"

Ava let out a kind of a *whoo hoo* noise and reached into her pocket and pulled out an old picture. "This is the picture we took up at the mission years ago."

Ivy looked over Ava's shoulder at the picture then stopped right in her tracks, letting out an audible gasp. "That's the picture, Ava! That's the one!" She was trembling. "I saw that picture and that place behind you," she pointed at the old mission, "and the hand sign! Ava, you sent me the hand sign!" Ivy's voice broke. "It was the final thing that give me the courage to come here."

Ava started to cry. "I don't know why I did that sign! I just hoped that maybe, somehow, you would see it in the future times and come here, and you did!"

With that, they hugged and cried the sweet tears of two dear friends reunited after a long travel and a very long time. The tears of finding out that after all that time, all that travel, that dearest of friends was still the same person, and you loved them just like you did in the before time and they loved you back. It was a happy-sad kind of feeling again. So happy to be together again and so sad it had taken so long to find each other.

"Girls, we have to go, I feel a darkness coming, and coming fast," Norah said softly, urging them on.

When they got to the mission steps, Norah went up them and went in. The girls stayed back at first, then Norah came out holding an old woman's hand. She led her down some steps to a bench where the girls joined them.

As they approached, the old lady started nodding her head like she knew them or knew about them. She started to talk but Ivy did not understand her, while Ava was transfixed.

Norah began to interpret for Ivy. "She is speaking Spanish, which she learned from the nuns while traveling here over the years. She said she can tell you are one of the travelers, just like her, just like us."

Ivy smiled at the old woman shyly, glad to be seen as one of them.

Ava helped translate as the woman spoke softly but firmly. "She said the travel changes you, makes you different, she can tell who is a traveler, the good ones and the bad."

Ava asked her a question in Spanish, and Norah continued interpreting as the woman answered.

"She says to go back, you have to go to the place where you arrived. To the exact place at the same time of day. But sometimes it doesn't work and she doesn't know why. Maybe you have more work to do before you leave. Maybe the trail is lost for a while. Her people have been using these trails from the beginning of their time. It is how they first came to this land from here across the seas when the sea could not be crossed."

Ava took over translating as the woman spoke. "She said you can also go down different trails, but you never know where they may lead. You have to be very careful or you could end up in the strangest of places…"

Here, the old lady paused, looking out in the distance, the wrinkles in her face deepening. To Ivy, she looked like was remembering things from long ago.

Then the woman began talking again as Norah translated. "She was a traveler, a healer, and did many travels to look for medicine. When her daughter died, she decided to be a traveler and look for help for other children. She has been to many places many times but this is the place she comes to the most. This is where her daughter lived with her all those years ago, so she likes to come to remember her. But sometimes she does not know what time it will be."

Ivy broke in, it was too much for her to keep silent any longer, she had so many questions. "What are these trails, these holes we call them? Where did they come from?"

The old lady smiled and went on, then Norah started to speak. "No one knows, they are from the time before people, they have always been here, and sometimes when the earth shakes, more trails open up and some close. There are many trails here, this is a special place, but the earth shakes a lot here and the trails are many."

Ava picked up where she left off. "Most people that travel here come for rest, they have had a hard life, a sad life and the gods bring them here to rest. But sometimes others come and they do not rest. They come looking for other travelers and sometimes they are hunters."

The old lady was looking right at Ivy now, and Ivy shivered as Ava spoke the woman's words.

"Keep away from the hunters! Sometimes traveling makes them crazy and they do bad things. Some learn how to use the trails better than others, these are the guides. They help the lost ones find a way home. There are even some guides that don't have to leave their time to travel the trails, they can do it right in their head."

Ivy jumped in at this excitedly. "I met one, I met one on the farm!" She felt like one piece of a giant puzzle had fallen into place.

The old lady then had a look of surprise on her face, as though the telling of the story made it seem more real to her than before.

Norah spoke for her now, quietly and sadly. "She feels strongly now that we must leave, all of us. She heard stories that some people are coming for us. They think we are bad medicine. They once thought this of her, but now there are people that want to hunt us in this place."

The old lady turned to Norah and spoke again quickly, urgently.

"What did she say?" Ivy asked, looking from Ava to Norah, who now looked more anxious.

Ava said, "She said it's time for us all to go, time to go back to our own time and finish the life we started there. She said we must leave very soon or something terrible will happen to us."

Norah added, "We have to go back to the tree, to the exact spot. She said that Ava is a guide, and that she has much traveling yet to do..."

Norah trailed off as the woman was still speaking, not wanting to tell Ivy all of it.

Ava turned pale. She understood the old lady and it made the blood drain from her face. A great evil was coming for them, not a mere evil, something much more. Death was coming and it would not be stopped. Ava and Ivy were more than just two young girls from a farm that fell into a hole. The holes had chosen them and the mission would be dangerous. Ava had been sent here on that mission, Ava was the key. A great evil was coming and together they would have to face it.

The old lady finished speaking and was taken away by the nuns to the *lavanderia* in front of the mission, a place where the washing of clothes was done for those at the mission. The nuns led the old lady right into the water, first reaching her knees then all the way up to her head. When she was fully underwater, she turned to look at the girls, eyes wide open and staring at them.

Ava watched, thinking the sight was so strange, the old lady not floating in the water but walking in it, fully submerged. She started to come back up, still staring at them. She gave a smile and an expression of great wonder and perhaps concern, then she took another step back under the water and disappeared. There one moment and then, no more, just gone.

The nuns clasped their beads and started to pray and rock back and forth. "El ángel se ha ido a casa otra vez." *The angel has gone home again.* As they prayed, they cried, not from sadness but from wonder. God had sent his angel to them and had taken her home again.

The color in Ava's face did not return for a long time. She did not know what the old lady meant, but she knew a great danger was coming, and more than that, to their lives. Something bigger than she could even imagine await-ed them. She, Ava, was to be a traveler and a guide! The thought of it filled her with fear. What did that even mean? What was she to do? Who had decided these things?

As they walked back home to their little shed, Ivy no-ticed Ava's skin had a curious subtle glow, something of her skin had changed. Ivy knew that something inside Ava had changed as well.

THE PRIEST

Just down the road from the shed, the shed full of life and hope and love, was another place. If there is an opposite to every force of nature, this was the opposite place to the shed.

In a tiny single-room church sitting on a lonely corner of the town, a priest sat on the floor by the pulpit. He was drunk again, full of rage for himself and for the people around him. Full of voices that were so loud he could not sleep. He swore this was the last time he would be drunk in his own church, but he had thought that many times. He was so full of rage. He prayed that the Lord would exact his revenge on all of these people that had wronged him.

He had looked through the passages of the Bible he loved so much, and what he saw was the God that smote, the God that raged and killed the Philistines, the God that killed the firstborn unless a sacrifice was made. He did not care for the passages about the God that turned the other cheek or asked "who among you is so innocent as to throw the first stone." That was not the God he followed.

He thought about how to make the people here understand that he was the hand of God in this place, that he was the avenging angel set to come to do God's work. In doing that work, he would make himself worthy of the love of God.

He had no love anywhere else. In fact, he decided long ago that being feared was better than being loved. A long time ago there had been a girl. He loved this girl, he wanted to make her his wife. He courted her and explained to her what a godly union it would be. He read to her the passages about how a woman must bow down to her husband, that the husband was the head of the household and what a great leader he would be for them.

When his words fell short and she refused him, he grew angry. She must marry him! How could she not? One night in his rage and his drinking he struck her, struck her hard and she ran off. The next day, her father arrived at his door with a gun in hand. He explained very clearly that his daughter never wanted to see him again and that if he tried, he would not hesitate to put a bullet in him, just one. Just one would do the job.

The priest had no doubt that he spoke the truth. The rage in him grew at this moment like he had never felt before. His own father had told him many times he was unlovable, as he struck him repeatedly and threw things at him. His father told him he would amount to nothing and no one wanted him. The priest took these beatings in stride, deciding they would make him strong. He took all that rage against him and made it his own, letting it simmer and grow inside. One day he would let the rage out and teach his father just how great his son really was.

He did see the girl again, found her alone and grabbed her by the arms so she could not escape. She told him she did not love him, did not ever want to be his wife, told him he was a bad man, a cruel man that only wanted a slave not a wife. The rage in him grew white hot, he wanted to strike her again and again but he did not. He had a better plan.

That night, he went to the tiny house where the girl and her family lived. As he prayed that his God would give him the strength to do what he knew was right, he barricaded the doors and windows as silently as he could. Around the dry wood house, he lit some rags soaked in oil and pushed them into gaps in the wood beams. He lit the rags, then slowly and with all the assurance of a man knowing he was doing God's work, walked away.

He was far off when he first heard the cries, the faint screams, and knew that he had cleansed the world of these unrepentant devils. It was then that he decided hate was better than love, he could hate anyone any time. Hate is what drove him and made him strong. Love was too hard, but hate came so easily.

Before the fire there were parts of him that wondered if he might be going mad. The voices in his head at times were so loud he could not sleep. Those same voices, though, told him of his greatness and his need to cleanse the world of the unbelievers. They told him often that he was the chosen one. They also belittled him and made fun of him, and when they were at their worst, this is when he would drink.

The drinking did not make the voices go away but it silenced them just a little so that he might sleep for a time. Though he was sure of the upright and righteous deed he had performed, he knew that the ignorant, unclean folks of the world would not understand and would jail him as they had done to this family.

So, he got on a train and set a path to the West, far from the people that had wronged him. And as he traveled, he dreamed of a church that would become the center of a God-fearing town with him as its head, the avenging angel God had sent to make the world right. He would bring the people of that town to the gates of heaven or hell, depending on what they chose for themselves. He would make it a righteous place right here on earth and he would be the priest and it would be good.

He was sure now, surer than ever, that men needed to have fear. Fear made men do the right thing. He also knew, now more than ever, that love was a weak thing, and that fear is what made men in the image of God.

The voices in his head told him to preach the word and to bring people out of their heinous ways and to turn to the God of fear. He found a place, a small town, a town ready for his words. He would preach in the main street to whoever would listen. He told the people of the town how they would surely bring on God's destruction if they did not change their ways. He told them of their sins of greed and lust. He told them of the weakness and ungodliness of the Indian and the Black man.

As he preached, he met with men that agreed with his ideas about the race of man and the Godly vision of the white man as leader and ruler of this new country. These men that called themselves a *Klan*, he thought he could come to lead them. And with them at his side, he could turn the whole town to God. With these men he raided many homes, burnt down many buildings, for this was not a place for the Indians or the Black man and they must leave. This was to be a town for the white man, and for God's plan, and he would lead the town to rightness.

He had not been in the town long when he started to hear stories of some women that had lived here a long time but did not seem to age. Some of the old folk swore they looked the same as they did all the years ago when they arrived. He heard these stories and knew that the Lord had come to test him. Again, the Almighty had sent women to test him!

He must find these women and make them subservient to him and his church. If they did not bow to him and become his wives, they would not be worthy of him and this place. They must be found! They must be made clean or else be cleansed from this place. He would know in an instant what would be their fate. He would find them, assess them, judge them, and if these devils did not measure up, they would be cleaned with fire. He had used fire before on a woman and it was good and right. He would show the town that he could bring these women to God and fear would be his weapon.

There was a child with them, a young child, and this he knew was a great danger. When the Lord sent a devil dressed as a child it made even the greatest follower hesitate in doing what must be done. But he would not hesitate— with a child or an adult, man or woman. He was the hand of God that would make this town free and rid it of any devil or threat to God's plan.

Even as he thought these things, his head hurt. The voices were so loud, so many. He drank his whiskey on the church floor so that he might clear his mind. He must go to these devils and drive them out. In front of the town he must burn them, as was the old way. He must excise these demons with fire if they did not bow down to him.

He would gather the men in the Klan and lead them in this crusade, and it would be holy and it would be good. And as he reached for another drink, he rubbed his temples and prayed to God to make the voices less loud and to bless his plan to find these devils and clean the town of them.

THE CHASE

Norah and the girls headed back to the shed as fast as they could. They were still a ways off when they heard the shouting. A small group of people had gathered at the front of the shed and were yelling for them to come out. They were dressed in weird white robes with pointed caps and some of them carried long clubs and knives. They could not make out what the people were saying, but the girls were scared.

"What are they saying? What is this?" Ivy asked anxiously.

"That is the Klan, Ivy, a hateful group of people that do nothing but make trouble. Seems they have joined our priest friend." Norah pointed near the front of the mob to a tall man with a long bread and a large pointed stick in his left hand, like a spear with a cross on the end, and a book in his right. He was leading a chant of some kind and the others were joining in.

The sight of it made Ava sick. She had seen these men before, seen what they had done to people in this town.

"The Klan?" Ivy asked, confused. "Like the KKK? I thought they were in Mississippi or Tennessee or something, not California.''

"I guess they're all over," Ava said, getting more anxious as she spoke. "I've seen them here with their robes and their torchers. And it never ends well. They're usually hating on the Black folk in town, but I think they hate just about everyone. I know I hate these people and I'm afraid of them. I've seen them do the most terrible things."

"Ava, we have to get Brett and Sharron out of the shed and get out of here," Norah declared.

Ava nodded, then said to Ivy, "There's a secret way into the shed we made years ago, for just a thing like this. It's behind the shed up on Victoria Street. We built a secret tunnel. It took us the longest time. Well, it mostly took Brett the longest time. It was his idea and he kept it secret for years until it was done."

"We have to get to the tunnel and get them out of there! Then we have to go to the tree and go home," Norah said, all the while watching the mob. "They are talking about us, Ava!'' she said. "I can make some of it out now. The priest in the front is calling for the witches to come out of the shed or they will burn it down. He is saying he has come to judge us. That much I heard."

With that, they backed out and made a loop around to the street called Victoria. The shed was large and hid them from the crowd in front. On Victoria Street was a series of small houses, one of them behind the shed, about thirty yards behind the fence that divided the properties.

Ava signaled them to stop and to stay as she moved like a ninja to the side of the house and lifted a small grate on the side. She disappeared for a moment, then poked her head out and signaled for them to come.

Norah and Ivy quickly and quietly made their way to the side of the house. It was getting dark already but the way was clear. Ava shuffled them under the grate and they found themselves in a crawl space under the house. On the far end of the crawl space was another grate.

Ava belly crawled her way to the grate and pulled it off, then reached inside and pulled out a lamp and a match and lit the lamp. Even before she lit the lamp, Ivy swore she saw a slight glow, a very faint light, coming from Ava herself. It was the most curious glow, subtle, but there. Ava's skin was glowing ever so slightly as to almost be missed, buy Ivy saw it.

As Ava lit the lamp, a group of rats that had been hiding behind an old block of wood went running in all directions. Ivy gave out a small shout and Norah immediately reached over and covered her mouth.

"We have to be quiet, Ivy! So quiet! Those rats won't hurt you. They want nothing to do with you," Norah whispered.

"Sorry," Ivy whispered back. "I'm not afraid of rats. We've got way worse stuff on the farm. Just scared the poop out of me, that's all."

They gathered themselves then headed for the second grate up near Ava.

"It's only about thirty yards to the shed but the tunnel is small, just big enough for one at a time," Ava quietly announced. "I'll go first with the lamp and you follow along. Once we get inside the shed, we'll get Brett and Sharron and come right back out before they burn it down."

Without another word, she headed down the tunnel and into the dark with only the lamp visible in the pitch black.

Ivy realized that Ava had indeed changed. On the outside she was still a thirteen-year-old-girl, but she talked, moved, and acted like a confident woman. And there was something more. Before Ivy could put her finger on the feeling, they were off to the shed.

The tunnel had a dirt floor and a wood ceiling, and every few feet wooden posts to hold up the roof. Ivy took a deep breath, she was not afraid of rats, that was for sure, but she was not very excited about being in such a small space. "Claustrophobia," that was what her teacher had called it. She had that a little, and it made her kind of panicky.

Yet when she thought about the men outside, all that had happened in just the last day... Had it really been just a day or two since Ava disappeared? Since she ran away and almost died in the river? Just a day since she found Norah's shed and gone to the ring tree and been transported here? Had this all happened so fast, and now this?

Knowing that Ava was leading them, she was able to move through the tunnel and not think too much about the walls falling in and being buried alive, though it did cross her mind. Before she had time to really get panicked, they arrived at the back of the shed. Ava had pushed open what looked like a small door but was in fact some kind of workbench with drawers.

They moved through the workbench and found themselves in a stable with a horse staring right at them. The horse looked confused, if a horse can actually do that. Ava stood up and gave the horse a pat on the head and whispered in its ear. The horse seemed to immediately relax and gave out a sweet neighing sound like a word of welcome.

Ivy was struck by this. There was something more than a horse greeting an old human friend here. She was a farm girl, she knew animals and people and how they acted toward each other. That horse *understood* Ava, like she had actually spoken to it in a language it recognized. Ava, her Ava, was still the same but also something very much more than she had been on the farm.

They moved through the stable and onto the stairs at the back of the shed. They could see a light coming from above, and as they made their way up, there at the top amongst the hay bales were Brett and Sharron waiting for them. They looked like they had been expecting them for a while. They had three small bags all packed and lanterns in their hands.

"Things are getting exciting here, ladies," Brett said. "Seems like our priest friend has joined a special club of dorks in white dresses and they have come to play." He was looking at Sharron as he said this and the rest knew what he was doing, making light of the situation so the child would not be scared.

Ivy thought it curious how Brett now spoke in two accents, using two languages. He seemed to flow between the Australian of his youth and the American of his old age.

He went on but in a soft voice. "I packed up some clothes and some bread and water for us and told Sharron you would be here soon and we were going on an adventure."

In the background they heard people banging on the barn doors and the horses were beginning to get agitated and starting to move around the stalls.

"Time to go," Norah announced and they headed back down the steps and to the tunnel entrance.

"Norah, you lead the way, I'll come last. I have to let the horses out before I go," Ava said quickly.

"But Ava, how long will that take? You might get caught if you open the doors!" Ivy protested.

"I'll be okay, the horses will cover me. Then I'll come right out. I cannot let them stay here and die if they light the place on fire. Now, go! They're getting louder, they mean business."

Ava stared at them and they knew there was no stopping her. They made their way to the tunnel as Ava headed back to the horses.

Ava had a plan, one she had thought about many times before. She knew, somewhere and somehow, this day would come. Trouble had been brewing for a long time. The people were getting more curious and more anxious as each year passed and they had not aged.

Then the priest had come, and while most of the people in town were not interested in his talk of devils and witches and the "coming end days," some were. Ava knew that one day, if Ivy did not come, the priest would, and they would have to flee.

Tonight was that night. She even guessed they would come with torches and burn the barn down. She had seen it before, seen what they had done to some folks in town and seen even worse when the people fled the buildings. She had seen it and had a plan.

She would gather the horses, all lined up as best she could, then she would open the doors where the men stood outside and let the horses go. In the confusion and the stampede, she would run with the horses and make her escape and meet the others by the fig tree.

She unlatched the gates to the horses' stall one at a time and with great speed. Each time she did, she whispered in the horses' ears something they seemed to understand, and they cocked their heads to the side. She had known all of them since before they were born, had fed and raised them right here. They knew her and she knew them.

Brett had said to Norah many times that he believed Ava could *actually* talk to them and them to her. It seemed crazy, but there was much about Ava that was not like other people, they all knew it. She was something different, and she was becoming more different every day.

Once she had opened the stall, she gathered all the horses into the center of the shed. She moved to the giant barn doors, then with all her might she pushed up the wooden plank that had held fast as the intruders tried to break it open. She gave out a shout, like a scream, but something else. Some who were there would later say it was a sound they would never forget, louder and more piercing than anything they had ever heard a human make.

With that scream the horses bolted, full speed, first to the door then out. Ava disappeared amongst the animals as they crashed through the half-open barn doors and through the gathered men in their white robes. The men scattered and fell and yelled. The priest was flung to the side by the lead horse, as if on cue. He let out a curse as he landed with a thump.

The horses first ran as one, then broke into smaller groups. Some headed into town and some toward the mountains.

Ava was nowhere to be seen. She had made her escape and was already headed to the tree near the ocean.

It was less than a mile to the old tree, but with little Sharron and elderly Brett it took some time. They saw that Ava had released the horses and that some were running through the streets of town and some up into the hills. It was a wonderful sign. The men in white had scattered and fallen and many were headed back into town, as if leaving a disappointing party that had taken a bad turn and they had decided to go to bed instead.

They rounded the turn at the bottom of State Street and headed across the beach front to the tree. They did not notice that a small group led by the priest had followed them down the road. Up ahead, they saw Ava waving to them to come quickly. It was dark out but the light of the moon made her visible.

Morning was now coming and they had to be quick. "Same time of day," the old lady had said and this was just about that time. Suddenly, Ivy was caught with the thought that they hadn't all come at the same time! *How can we leave at the same time? Will it still work? What are the rules of this game?* She had a sense of fear and dread, that it was all too much, and maybe wasn't even real. Yet in this moment, it sure felt real.

As they approached Ava, they saw that she was staring not at the tree, but off to the side of the tree.

"What are you looking at, Ava?" Ivy asked. The look on Ava's face was one she had never seen before and Ivy had seen them all.

"I can see the holes, Ivy! I can see them now! Another one is coming, right there, can you not see it?" Ava pointed to a black part of the field next to the tree.

Ivy looked hard and thought maybe she could see something, but decided it must be in her head. "No, Ava, I don't see anything," she confessed.

"It's very faint, but it's coming fast, moving toward this place and time. It will be here soon," Ava said in a trance-like state.

"What is it? Where is it coming—"

But before Ivy could finish, she was interrupted by the sound of men yelling after them. They turned and saw the men coming with their clubs, and the priest with that spear.

Brett, Norah, and Sharron had made their way to the tree and were climbing up one of the limbs. Brett motioned for them to come, a panicked look on his face.

The men were closer now, and Ava could feel the hate, like sweat, pouring out of them. She had not felt this before, but it was as real as anything she had felt. It came off the priest in thick waves. The other men seemed mostly just excited to be on a hunt.

Ava and Ivy ran to the tree. As Ava looked up into the canopy of branches, she could see the hole. A silvery dark hole with what looked like a million stars inside. She did not know how she could see it, but as she looked closer, she saw the farm and the kookaburra and she realized she could feel where the hole went.

With quick bounds, Ava and Ivy made it to the tree limb, as the men were very close now. The stink of hate coming off the priest was toxic to Ava. She looked back and the hole had started to move in a pulsating manner as if timing something.

She turned to Norah and Sharron. "You have to go now! This leads back to your time and ours, but you have to go exactly when I say."

It was the first time that Norah understood, really felt, they were from different times, these five. She and Sharron were not from their time and it was time to go back.

Ava looked at Norah in a most loving and tender way. "I can get you back to the time at the river, but a little early, just before your husband dove in the water." She spoke softly now. "You can save him, Norah. Do you want that?"

Norah's eyes welled up with tears. "Is that possible?" she asked. "Yes, I would do anything for that, Ava. There has not been a day in all these years that I haven't wished I could have gotten there a little faster. I know I could have saved him." Norah wept now, thinking of it.

"I can get you there, Norah, I can see the hole. I can see its pulse and I can time it so you go back to that time," Ava said.

"How, how is that possible?" But Norah knew there were things that she would never know, and right now Ava was something she had never seen before and was becoming something even more right in front of her. This young lady she loved like a daughter was more than a regular girl. She had always known it, but recently it had become more obvious.

Norah hugged Ava, held her so very tight, as Sharron joined her. "Will we see you again?" Norah asked.

Ava looked up with a most curious look. "Yes, I know we will see each other again." She smiled even as she said it.

The men had arrived at the base of the tree and were starting to throw rocks at them.

"Now, Norah! You have to go now!" Ava declared.

Norah had already reached out for Brett and given him the most tender kiss on the cheek. "Thank you for everything, Brett!" she said as Sharron held onto his hand.

While this was going on, Ivy slipped something into Norah's pocket without her noticing. Then, before they even knew what was happening, Ava shoved Sharron first, then a moment later from behind, Norah. Off the tree limb they went, and they were gone.

There was no time to even be amazed, as more rocks had started flying.

Ava looked back at the hole. "Our time is soon, get ready!" She turned to Brett, "Are you sure you want to go back, Brett? Back to that place and time?"

Brett nodded. "It's time. I've had a long life here, but I would like to go back and see it one more time…" As he said it, he did not look at Ava, he was staring at Ivy. Then he asked, almost pleading, "Could I go back to the time when we were kids, Ava?"

"No, Brett, there is a thing you have to do. I think you know it. You have to go back with Ivy and me," Ava said, but Brett did not notice her lips move.

Brett looked back at Ivy, and Ava knew what she saw in his eyes. It was love. Brett had loved Ivy since they were the smallest of kids. Ava knew then that some love really does last a lifetime, even a lifetime apart.

Before she could take that thought one more step, she was hit by a rock and taken back into the real world. She looked over the field and gasped, "Oh my!" She could see it coming—a new hole, coming fast—and when it got here, all hell would break loose in this place.

"Get ready! On my count, we jump! Another hole is coming and it will shake the earth, but we have to get the timing just right so wait for me!" she yelled to Ivy and Brett over the shouts below and a curious thundering in the distance.

Then the earth started shaking, at first a little, then a lot, then a whole lot more.

Faint cries could be heard from the town as the earth seemed to be rolling under them, but the tree held firm.

"Witches!" came a cry from below and Ava knew it was the priest. In his hand was a homemade spear shaped like a cross. It was very old and very large, and cocked and ready to be released even as he was losing his footing.

From the town came more cries as buildings were falling and chaos erupted. This was an earthquake and it was a big one. The old buildings in the town did not stand a chance and started to fall like dominoes. First the store fronts, then entire buildings. People were running, screaming, all hell had indeed broken loose.

Ava looked back at the tree and the hole that hovered just below the branch. "Okay, hold my hands and follow me in just a few seconds!" she called out.

As they readied for their escape, Brett looked down and saw the priest had released his spear. It was headed right at Ivy.

"Now!" Ava yelled and they jumped down, but Brett moved first to his left as he went. A sharp pain in his side gave way to a blistering light and speed that he had not forgotten in all these years. It was the same light and speed as when he had fought under the water decades ago, fought to catch his breath as he was sure he was about to die.

A second later that could have been a year, or ten, or an instant, the three travelers landed with a thump on the ground. The sounds and smells immediately changed, the sea was gone, the earth was quiet. No movement, no rocking, no cries from far off. A kookaburra gave out a laugh as they landed.

Ava looked up and back at the sky, and there in the ring of the tree was a silvery orb, as clear as day. She could not understand how she had not seen it all those years before.

Ivy and Brett were making their way to their feet. Brett turned to Ava and said, "Did we do it? Are we back on the farm?"

"We did. It's the time after you left, after you went under the water. Everyone in this time thinks you're dead." Ava gave him a small smile, as if to say she was sorry.

"That's not a bad thing, Ava. I had a good long life, but I needed to come back here one last time."

They all started to walk, and even without speaking, they all knew where they were going. Behind them, an object they did not see in their excitement of arriving lay pulsing like the hole.

The walking was slow, as Brett seemed to drag more the longer they went. Then they saw it, the bend in the river where Brett had disappeared. He was barely moving now and he sat down by a tree near the very spot he loved so much from the past. Ava and Ivy sat next to him.

As they sat, Ivy reached her hand up to steady Brett then looked down, puzzled by what she found. "Brett, you're bleeding!" On Brett's left side was a blood-soaked area on his shirt.

"I think the priest got me with that spear," Brett said, as though it were a small thing and nothing to worry about.

"We have to get you a doctor, Brett, there's so much blood!" Ivy declared anxiously.

"No time for that. This is my time, this is the place I wanted to come back to one last time," Brett said with a sense of complete calm. He looked at Ivy with the eyes of his younger self. "You will not believe this, Ivy," he started, "I dreamed about this exact moment years ago. I dreamed it like it just happened! I dreamed that someone was going to hurt you and I had to stand in the way."

His voice was getting weaker as he went on. "I didn't have a happy life here except for you two. I dreamed that I saved you when I was a kid and that made my whole life worthwhile. It was like this was my job, the most important thing I would ever do. Now look at this, here it is, what a thing is that..." He started to drift off.

Ivy was crying now. "Oh, Brett no, you can't go again. I can't take it, you already died once. Please, not again," she begged through her tears.

He was barely audible now. "But I didn't die, Ivy. I went on a most excellent trip. Now I got to come home, so I'm happy. I love you, Ivy, always have. Now it's your time to live," he whispered.

Ivy and Ava sobbed as Brett closed his eyes with a smile.

Home Again

Without words, but with full understanding, the girls made a burial place for Brett right under the tree. It was his favorite part of the farm. Something about the turn in the river and how you could see at a distance as the river came and went was like no other place on the farm.

You could also see his house up on the hill. He often liked to look at it, but he did not like to go back to it. He would often sit here for hours, even before the girls came to play for the day when they were children. He would think about the house, he would think about all manner of things, but mostly he would think about Ivy.

As they did their sad work, both girls had to stop to cry and hug more than once when the emotions became too heavy to bear.

"He's resting now, Ivy. He worked so hard, protected us so well for all those years," Ava said.

"Couldn't you go back and save him, Ava? You seem to be able to go to other times and places now, like you did for Norah," Ivy asked, expecting the answer.

Ava shook her head. "I don't know how it all works, but I know it's dangerous. I thought about it. When I looked through the hole, I saw the bird and it shook its head. I got the message, some things are too dangerous to do too often."

She slumped down. "I don't know what's happening to me. I'm scared. I don't want it. I can see things now, hear things, it's happening fast now and it scares me..." she trailed off.

"I know," said Ivy. "I can see it. There's something changing in you. But I'm here, Ava." Ivy was full of sorrow now, knowing things would never be as they were. She knew that things change with young girls as they become women, and they *were* getting older, but this was some-thing more.

Ava looked at Ivy as if she could read her thoughts. "This is our time, Ivy. We're growing up, becoming wom-en. I think we're going through a bigger change than we can even imagine."

Ivy nodded sadly, then cried out, "Brett saved me, Ava! I think he jumped in front of that spear!" Only now realizing how very brave Brett had been on her behalf.

"He did, Ivy, he saw it coming and he moved to save you," Ava said in a small, sad voice. "He saw that spear coming a lifetime ago. He saw that to save you he would have to die and he waited a lifetime to do it."

Ivy just sat, there were no more tears. She was exhaust-ed from all that had happened. She missed her mother, she missed Brett, she missed the old life before everything went wrong. She thought about how things would never be the same. How she would never look at the farm, or the ring tree, or the native people or anything the same again.

She now knew things most people would never know. And she knew of love. A boy who had become a man and grown old had waited an entire life to save her. And she knew hate. That angry mob, that priest was filled with hate, and like Ava, she felt it.

"What do we do now?" Ivy asked. "Where do we go now?"

"I'm not sure, but we're back just a day after you left. Maybe you should go home just to show your mom you're alive," Ava suggested. "I know she's not a good mother but it is a terrible thing to lose someone like that. I think you should go back, even if just for a short time."

Ava paused, looking far off into the distance, her thoughts in another place now as she spoke. "I think I have to go back to the ring tree. I think there is something I have to do."

Ivy shook her head no, but before she could protest, Ava continued, more firmly.

"Yes, Ivy. There is something here that should not be here, not in this place, not in this time. I have to send it back. I'm not sure what it is but I know I have to send it back."

Ivy saw there was no changing Ava's mind, and with that, the girls agreed to the work set before them and to meet back at the bend in the river after it was done.

Ivy walked toward the house, the old familiar feeling immediately upon her. It was always the same way. She at once felt sad for the days when that house was a happy place, then angry, even scared, at what it had become.

Ivy did not know the whole story, only that her father had left and so had Ava's mother. That is when Ava came to live with them. Nothing was ever the same after that. Ivy loved Ava and always had, but the very presence of them both together made Ivy's mother very sad and angry.

She often yelled at them, telling them this was all their fault. She started drinking more and more and was drunk now from morning until night. She stopped caring for herself and for the girls. It was a terrible thing for a young girl to watch, her mother coming apart in front of them.

Yet even then, at the worst of it, Ivy knew somewhere in there was her other mother, the mother that loved her and played with her in the happy time. Somewhere in there was a mother's love. She now knew something about love and what it could do. She wondered if she might be able to help her mother come back to them, to unlock the love that she was now sure was still inside her. She had learned that love can last more than a lifetime.

As she got closer to the house she heard crying, long loud sobs. It sounded more like an animal than a person.

"She's gone! Oh my God, she's gone!" Ivy's mother screamed into the air with all the pain of an insight that is too much to bear. "My girl has gone, what have I done?"

When Ivy walked through the door, her mother looked up, first confused, then surprised, then something like relief or regret spread across her face. She ran to Ivy and hugged her longer and harder than Ivy could ever remember.

"I'm so sorry, Ivy! I'm so sorry! I thought you had run away! I've been a terrible mother," Ivy mother confessed though the tears. She pulled away suddenly, looking into Ivy's face. "Where's Ava? I've been such a terrible mother to you both!" she cried. "I'm so sorry. I've been so sad, so angry, but when I thought I had lost you *both* it was too much."

Ivy's mother hugged her again even as she pleaded with Ivy to forgive her. "I will be better, Ivy. I'll be back now. I'll be back from that bad place and we can be a proper family."

Ivy was filled with sadness and regret of her own, but mostly she felt love. She understood that her mother was indeed back, there was something about the size of the pain, the realization of the pain, that made Ivy know it was more powerful than the sadness and the anger. For the first time in a very long time, Ivy's mother stood without wobbling, spoke without slurring. For the first time in a very long time, Ivy saw her mother, the old one she had lost.

* * *

As Ava approached the ring tree she saw a figure nearby. A man, dark skinned, one of the original ones. She had seen him before around here, just passing through, walking quietly among the trees and the animals, but today he stood silently near the tree. He did not speak but Ava knew to go to him.

Getting closer, she saw what she did not know she was looking for. On the ground next to the man was a spear, glowing at the tip. It made her feel uneasy.

"Should not be here, full of hate, that one," the man said quietly. "Send it back that one, send it back," he said while looking at Ava with a kind and knowing but intense face. "It should not be in this place. Send it back, little one."

Then he turned and walked away.

Ava stopped for a few moments, then looked up and called after him.

"How do I send it back?" she pleaded.

The way it came, send it the way it came. Ava heard the voice in her head, even though the man was now too far away to be heard. She heard him as clear as if he was standing next to her.

Ava looked down at the spear, saw that it was pulsing. Pulsing with anger and rage and it scared her. She looked up at the tree and the hole within the ring and she knew what to do. She picked up the spear and immediately dropped it. It was hot, but that was not why she dropped it.

It was full of hate, dripping with it, pulsing with so much hate. It was an evil thing; she could feel it.

She did not want to pick it up again, but once more the voice came. *Send it back.* She turned and expected to see the man next to her but he was far off now.

Again, she reached down and picked up the spear. The feeling returned but this time she was ready. The hate, the anger, seemed to want to crawl out of the spear right up her arm and into her. With her mind she pushed it back, pushed it back into the spear.

Then, with fresh energy, she ran toward the tree, fast, then faster still. She gave out a cry, and with the pulsing of the spear and the hole timed just right, she flung the spear up at the ring tree.

Far away, in her house, Ivy heard a loud almost deafening crack, like lightning, then felt a shock wave that threw her to the floor. Ivy's mother fell as well, both of them stunned, lying on the floor.

"What was that!" her mother called out.

Ivy did not answer but she knew Ava had something to do with it.

As though her mother sensed it too, she asked anxiously, "Where is Ava, Ivy? I must see her! I must talk to her!"

"She's at the ring tree."

And even as Ivy said it, she knew the noise had come from there. She knew Ava had found the thing she was looking for. She knew what Ava had done—she could feel it, she could even see it. And as she saw these things, she felt a cold shiver, then something like relief. Something lifted in the air, a feeling she had not even known she had felt. Something like a lightness in the air had come.

EPILOGUE

Ava and Ivy sat on a blanket down by the river. "They found Brett's body, Ava, did you hear? Except they didn't know it was him, they said it was an old man, buried under a tree where Brett disappeared. Do you think they'll figure out it's him?" Ivy asked, staring off into the distance.

"Not sure they ever will. They're looking for a boy, not an old man."

"Will we ever see him again?" Ivy asked in a sad quiet voice. "I would love to see him again. I can't imagine not seeing him again," she continued, even sadder now.

There was a long pause as Ava looked out over the river. "Think we will, but before then, I have to go back to Santa Barbara, to that time again. There's something I have to do."

Ivy stared at her, shocked, not knowing what to say for a moment.

Ava took a deep breath. "It's the priest, Ivy, I have to go find him. But I think I'll see Brett there again."

"I'm coming, Ava. I'm coming with you. I'm not leaving you again," Ivy said quietly, but in a tone that did not require an answer. It was decided.

* * *

Norah landed with a start but began running even before she could take a step. Sharron was not with her, and she knew why. She sprinted with all her strength toward the river. There was no pain in her, no fatigue, only panic. She moved faster and faster as she approached the river.

Norah had lived this scene before, many, many years ago. She had lived on the banks of the river for five years with her husband. He was a good and kind man, a man that had grown tired of the work of running a paddle boat and decided to take his chance at farming the land instead. They had met down by the river and were immediately taken with each other.

He would tell her of his plans to farm the land and settle down and have a family. She told him of her work in the hospital, of learning to be a nurse, and how she would like to return to the river and be a local district nurse, helping the people from her community since it took too long to get to the local hospital.

As they told each other of their dreams, the dream became one. Then they became one and were married. He would farm the small piece of land he could afford, she would open a tiny clinic at the river's bend, and together they would start a new life together.

A few years later, Sharron was born and she was the center of their universe. As much as they loved each other, their love for Sharron was even greater. It was a shared love that brought them even closer as parents, and like all good partners, the love they felt for each other was felt by Sharron and it made them all strong and happy.

Then came that day down by the river Norah could never forget, even after an entire lifetime had passed. Norah, like most parents, greatly feared the bad things that could happen to her child. At times, she had to push the horrible thoughts from her mind as it was too sad, too terrifying. It was a foreboding kind of joy to stand over your sleeping child and feel so much love, yet at the same time be so scared that something could happen to them that would tear out your heart and soul.

While she feared for Sharron in this way, she did not think tragedy would come for her husband, and yet it did.

On that morning, she sat at her table reading an old medical book, trying to take it all in, and watched in terror as Sharron, playing next to the river's edge with her husband right next to her, fell into the river. Sharron was just learning how to swim but she had not yet learned the trick to staying above water, to let it hold you up while you moved over the top. As she slid under the water, Norah's husband spun around, and without thought or hesitation, dove into the water.

Both were gone now as Norah jumped up and ran toward the water, seeing the most curious sight as Sharron came shooting out of the water onto the river's edge. Somehow, her husband must have ejected her out from under the water to save her life, but he was nowhere to be seen.

She went first to Sharron to see that she was indeed okay, then turned to the water and still saw no sign of her husband. In a panic, she rushed to the water's edge and walked in, searching for him with her arms and feet while keeping both eyes on Sharron so she could stop her if she slipped again.

For an instant, just one tiny instant, she felt something soft, something she knew was her husband. But even as she reached down, he was gone. This river with all its dead trees and caverns and underwater currents had taken the man she loved away.

She did not stop looking and searching for the longest time until exhaustion and her crying child made her finally stop. For days, then weeks then months, she searched for him but he never appeared, alive or dead. He was simply gone and perhaps this was the worst part.

Now, as she ran back to this place again after all these years, an entire lifetime, the events of that horrible day fueled her speed. She would not let that happen again, she could not! She had been given a second chance, a second chance that the world never gave when death was final and that was that. Yet here it was, another chance to get her life back, to save the man she so desperately loved, the father of her child, the very reason for her life. This time she would not, could not, fail.

She did not slow at the river's edge; she dove in at full speed at the place just below their cabin. As she did, she saw that Sharron, who was playing at the river's edge, had slipped on a branch and tumbled into the river. Norah saw her go under and saw her husband spin around at the sound of it.

Norah swam giant strokes to the place Sharron had slipped in just as her husband hit the water. With one hand, Norah grabbed Sharron, and with the brute strength of a protective mother, pulled her up and threw her onto the bank.

As if in slow motion, Norah saw Sharron crying but safe on the bank. Then she saw herself running toward the water, right to where she was now, but in an instant, she was gone. And like a cool breeze she felt this version of herself enter her body. She was now this time's Norah, the two had become one.

All this happened in an instant, and now Norah spun back to the water but her husband was nowhere to be seen. She dove underneath, searching with her hands in the muddy water, not finding anything.

She needed to come up for a breath and was in a total panic when her foot hit something soft, not a tree, not a branch, but a person. She plunged further down and her hands confirmed it was her husband, his clothes caught on a submerged branch even as he tried to get them off. She pulled and ripped at the seams. She knew exactly where to pull; she had made these clothes and knew how to un-make them.

With one giant yank, she pulled off his shirt and pushed him up to the surface. He gasped and coughed and fell toward the bank, Norah following right behind him.

"Sharron, where is she!" As he said it, Sharron came down the bank crying and scared and grasping at them both.

Norah rolled onto her back, one arm around Sharron and one around her husband, as a lifetime of sadness and loss was released and turned into joy.

Later, Norah would reach into her pocket and find a piece of paper. Except it was not paper. It was a wet but clear photograph of all of them at the mission. She held it to her heart and kept it with her until she died, many years later, an old and happy woman, in that same cabin.

* * *

As the priest pushed himself up, he heard a loud crack over the rumbling of the ground and trembling of the earth below. Had he hit her? It was a perfect throw, he must have hit her. *Hit the little witch, killed the little witch.*

Even as he thought these things, out of thin air came his spear. The same one he had just thrown as the devils disappeared. It was coming right back at him, fast. He had no time to move out of its path.

The spear hit him in the side with such force it sent him flying onto his back, though he did not even have time to feel it. He was out before he hit the ground.

NOTES AND DISCLAIMERS

While the characters and incidents in this book are purely fictitious, many of the places and historical events are real and based on actual events. Here are some things you might be interested to know:

- There is a ring tree near Tooleybuc, NSW, Australia.
- There is a place in Santa Barbara, California, where a tree planted by an Australian girl over 100 years ago remains today. It is a Morton Bay Fig and it is enormous.
- Santa Barbara once had an equestrian shed on a street now called Equestrian. Where that shed once stood there is now a magical home, but that is another story.
- The KKK did have a chapter in that same town in the 1920s and 30s.

- An earthquake destroyed most of the town the morning of June 29, 1925.
- A Chinese ship crashed into the Santa Barbara Wharf in the 1800s.
- Albert Einstein rested and rode a bicycle in Santa Barbara nearly 100 years ago.
- Santa Barbara is a magical place, and mysterious and wonderful people live there today.
- There is a farm called "Norah Bend" in Australia on a river called the Murray. Norah apparently lived there near a bend in the river. A number of young people died in that river over the years, some were never found.
- There is a "Central School" near the farm in this story, like the one Ava, Ivy, and Brett attended.
- Tooleybuc is a real place and the farm in this story is indeed real.

About the Author

Mel Herbert was born in Australia and grew up on a farm in the "outback." He often spent his days roaming the thousands of acres of the farm and coming up with stories and imaginings. He dreamed of far-off lands and a world of science fiction. He went on to become a physician and traveled the world, seeing extraordinary things and meeting amazing people. He has lived and worked in the United States for over 30 years, but will always be the kid from that farm with the wonderful birds and kangaroos.